Kissing Chaos

A Small Town, Friends to Lovers Romance

EM Chandler

EM Chandler Books LLC

Contents

For my elevator mechanic—thank you for your part in making this dream a reality.

This book contains the following:

FMC with anxiety and ADHD

Cheating (off-page, not main characters)

Death of a parent and of a partner (off-page)

Pain pill addiction (not detailed, secondary character)

Use of alcohol

Know your limits. Your mental health matters.

— EM Chandler

CHAPTER ONE

Jett

"Come on, come on, come on," I mumble as I wait for this slow-as-molasses elevator. The temptation to press the call button again is almost too much.

My therapy appointment is in less than five minutes, and I look like a wet dog standing in the lobby of this Atlanta high rise. I should have stayed in bed. This is my punishment for thinking traffic would have died down by ten in the morning.

It didn't.

I even woke up early thanks to the rumbling of thunder shaking the house. Although, the being-ahead-of-schedule thing may have been the problem. False sense of security and all. I thought I had enough time to fix breakfast, so I threw together eggs, sausage, and a piece of toast.

It turns out reading while I cook and eat is a bad idea. I got lost in the pages of Siena Trap's most recent hockey romance and forgot I had to leave the house. Then the I-285 connector was a nightmare, because no one knows how to drive in the rain.

Again, I should have expected it. I'm a Georgia girl, through and through.

When I finally arrived at my therapist's office, the parking lot was full, so I had to park four blocks away and run to the building.

In the rain.

Without an umbrella.

Because why would I remember to grab the one I set by the door last night after checking the weather three times? Total craziness, I know.

And now this elevator is moving slower than a dial-up connection.

I sigh in relief as a ding finally signals the elevator's arrival and the light on the call button turns off. I rush through the doors as soon as they open, turning and pressing the twenty-seven and then spamming the close button, all while cursing McKenna for forcing me to schedule this appointment for today. Groaning quietly, I shake my head at the overexaggeration.

I need this session. I know I do.

Stupid Joey. Stupid me for wasting two years with him. The worst part? I'm obsessing over what *I* did wrong.

What did you do wrong, Jett?

Nothing. Not a damn thing.

I have yet to give my best friend any details about what happened the day my ex left. I understand my brain well enough to know that I should talk to someone sooner rather than later, but I'm just not ready to share any of this with someone I know.

At least not with McKenna.

Definitely not with my brother, the only other constant in my chaotic life. Those are the only two people I could talk to. How sad is that? My dad doesn't need the stress of his grown daughter's breakup when he is two states away. My mom would just try to force me into more therapy if I mentioned my state of mind.

As the doors of the elevator close behind me, I lean my head back against the metal wall, taking long, slow breaths. The quiet instrumental music sounds like something from my teenage years, and I can't help but nod along to the beat, letting some of the tension slip from my shoulders. No one was paying the weird, wet girl any attention in the lobby, but my brain is convinced that everyone was judging me.

Like anyone would want to look at this hot mess.

I tap my foot to the beat of the music pouring out of the speakers, relaxing more with each passing floor until the song cuts off mid-note. The elevator shutters a few seconds later and comes to a sudden halt, jarring me into the control panel. At first, I assume someone is about to get on with me. I close my eyes and lean against the back wall, willing myself to breathe through the anxiety of sharing a small space with random strangers. Except, why would the music have stopped?

My heart races against my chest at the realization that the elevator is no longer functional. I'm trapped in this metal death can. I slam the call button with my palm, but nothing happens. I press it again. And again.

My fingers tangle into my hair, pulling on the loose strands.

"No, no, no, no, no. This is not happening right now."

Slipping my phone out of my back pocket, I'm torn between calling McKenna to panic or contacting the office a few floors above. It's pointless, though, as there is zero cell service in here. Zilch. Nada.

Desperate, I hit the alarm button. A shrill chime fills the metal contraption and the surrounding elevator shaft. I pace in the small space, counting my steps while trying to keep my breathing even. Three steps across, pivot, three steps back. I hate that it's an odd number, but changing the rhythm of my footfalls to adjust the number of steps feels too unnatural.

"Well, Jett. If you'd stuck with your plans out of high school to move to Kentucky and open a bookstore, you wouldn't be in this mess," I mumble to myself. "You could be living a quiet life in racehorse country instead of dealing with heartbreak."

One hundred seventeen steps around the elevator later, a literal voice from above nearly scares the shit out of me.

"Anyone in there?" the deep, gruff voice asks.

"Yep," I squeak, a hand clinging to my chest in an attempt to keep my pounding heart from taking a leap.

"Anyone injured or need medical assistance?"

I blink a few times, still trying to fight off the uneasy feeling of being trapped in this tube of death. "Um, no. I'm the only one in here. Scared shitless and could use a shot of whiskey, but I'm not injured."

It sounds like the guy chokes back a laugh. I'm glad someone finds me funny, because I sure as hell don't.

"Lucky for you, I was a few floors above you working on a different issue. Same elevator bank, so I heard the chime as soon as you triggered the alarm."

"Lucky isn't the word I'd use," I say breathlessly as the singular thought of being trapped continues swirling around my brain. Trapped. In a metal box. Hundreds of feet up. "If you were close, why'd it take you so long to get over here?"

A solid thunk above me triggers the most undignified squeal—I don't have anyone or anything to blame it on except that my nerves are shot.

"No reason for panic, ma'am. Storm just knocked out the power, and the generator didn't transfer. Besides, ten minutes is better than the two hours it'd take the fire department, yeah? I'm going to drop onto the roof of the cab so that I can open the doors and help you step out, okay? The elevator may shake some, but you're safe."

I hum a response but still jump a little when I hear and feel him land on the roof above me.

"Still with me, ma'am?"

"Mmm, yep."

"Want me to walk you through what I'm doing?"

"Sure. Why not?" Mumbling more to myself than to him, I add, "Nothing else to do."

He chuckles, his voice trickling down to me. "Are you always this spicy? Or just today? You're stuck between floors, so I'm going to disable the door restrictor and then manually roll open the car doors. You're only a few inches above a floor, so you'll be able to just step out."

Moments later, the doors to this stupid contraption open to the most ruggedly handsome man I have ever seen.

"Holy fireballs."

The words slip out before I can stop them. He looks at me somewhat perplexed, like there's no way he heard me correctly. But hot damn, this guy is worth looking at. If he were a book boyfriend, his defined, scruff-covered jaw and dark, chocolate eyes would melt the panties right off the female lead in any less-freakishly terrifying moment. Even covered in what looks like soot, this guy is love-interest quality. Dark-brown hair peeks out from the ball cap he's sporting, and his cotton uniform shirt clings to mile-wide shoulders. I wonder what they'd be like between—

No, Jett. Do not go there.

He's not insanely tall—maybe five-foot-ten—but the space he consumes makes me feel tiny in comparison. I swear I am trying to keep my eyes on his face, but they apparently have a mind of their own as they roam my rescuer's fine form. When I finally force them up north, I nearly choke on an embarrassed laugh as I realize he is staring at me with a mix of what I think is amusement and bewilderment.

Damn it, Jett. Quit staring.

I clear my throat before finding my voice. "Thanks for, you know"—I motion behind me at the still-open elevator—"that, and all. Though I guess it's probably part of your job. Otherwise, how would you know that stuff, right?" I groan, darting my eyes all around us, terrified of landing them on the scrumptious man who just saved me. "Sorry, I ramble when I'm nervous. Or stressed. Or really any time."

Shut. Up. Jett.

"Noah." The tin can hero holds out his hand as he introduces himself. "And it is in my job description, but you are very welcome."

I slip my hand into his much larger, much rougher hand for only a moment before I pull back and begin fidgeting with the hem of my shirt.

So late. So, so late.

Shit. McKenna is going to kill me. Not really—she loves me too much—but we made a deal last night that I would make it to this appointment today and she would ask the single dad of one of her preschoolers out for coffee. I want my best friend to find her person even if I can't find mine.

I need to get upstairs. And far away from this hunk of a man before my brain turns to mush and I make a fool of myself by drooling.

"I need to get up to the twenty-seventh floor. Where is the staircase?" I rush, looking around.

He points to the door at the end of the elevator bay. "Through that door. Each flight is numbered, so you shouldn't have any issue finding twenty-seven."

I thank him and practically race to it. As the door to the staircase closes behind me, I can't help but think that I wouldn't mind running into Noah again.

***

"I am sorry, Miss Taylor. You missed your session by over half an hour, and our next opening isn't until tomorrow."

Of course, the power was restored while I was racing up the stairwell, so the computers were up and running in my therapist's office by the time I made it to their floor.

"I've been here, though," I plead, my hands clenching and unclenching as I try, and fail, to keep it all together. "I was stuck in the elevator and had to wait for help."

"I understand that, ma'am. However, we only had a thirty-minute appointment set for you today, and the patient following you was on time for hers."

My eyes close in defeat, the weight of all the recent drama in my life once again crushing me. My voice is nearly a whine as I ask, "Is anyone else available to meet with me today? I'll wait all day if I have to."

The receptionist looks at me with a mix of pity and annoyance but sighs before scrolling through the appointment app on her computer. The second sigh that leaves her lips tells me everything I need to know. "I am sorry, but it looks like everyone is booked up."

My shoulders slump as my chin trembles, this morning's insanity finally clashing with my own chaotic thoughts.

I'm making my way toward the door when the receptionist takes pity on me and says, "There is a psychiatrist who offers emergency sessions in the afternoons, if you want her contact information."

Can I set the month of January on fire, please?

Anxiety rages war on my stomach and pulse as I try to accept my reality that I am now one of those patients needing an emergency mental health session. Nibbling on my bottom lip, I nod. Pinky promises are serious business.

I can do this.

"Where is she located?"

"Havenwood."

I jolt back a little. "Havenwood?"

The receptionist nods, oblivious to my shock. "Yes, ma'am. If you make your way to I-20 and—"

"My brother lives in Havenwood. You mean to tell me that I've had a closer option within this practice for the last two years?"

"Miss Taylor, Dr. Kristen Flynn just recently transitioned to a small personal office. She is technically no longer a partner in this practice, but I can assure you she is wonderful at her job.

And she keeps afternoons open for those individuals who find themselves in unexpected situations." Her smile is reassuring, though my heart and head are anything but.

Reassured, that is.

The thought of someone new seeing inside my head is daunting. I've seen the same therapist for the last two years, having only recently admitted to some of my more intimate struggles. The ones my family doesn't know about.

What is there to see? Depression and a solid thunk when I hit rock bottom?

Eyes clenched shut, bottom lip firmly between my teeth, I nod again. "I'll take the number." No point in putting off the inevitable.

***

The trembling in my fingers almost has my phone falling to the ground as I dial Dr. Kristen Wilson-Flynn's office. I haven't made it to the stairwell yet—no way am I getting back on the elevators after the massive failure earlier. Though I wouldn't mind running into that mechanic from earlier again. I have a feeling he'll be embedded in my memories for a while.

As the phone line rings, I steel myself for someone to answer. If I wait until I am in my car, I'll chicken out. Calling strangers, scheduling appointments—I prefer to do all of that online. No need to have human interactions when it isn't necessary.

Maybe that sounds a little too hermit-y.

If the shoe fits...right?

People make me nervous. I never know how to interact with strangers, and I always zone out into a daydream when I should be following along with whatever story or tidbit is being shared.

I've never been good at friendships or relationships—not being mentally present, creating stories when I should be focusing on any given task, and not hearing what anyone says until their words process a few seconds later doesn't lead to deep connections. It wasn't until I was twenty-three and struggling with a college assignment during my final semester that I finally talked to someone about my lack of focus—or rather, hyper focus on the wrong thing—and completed an ADHD assessment. Tada. Two decades of struggles explained in an hour.

The phone in my hand quits ringing before a motherly voice travels through the speaker. "Dr. Wilson-Flynn's office. This is Willa. What can I do for you?"

Words stick in my throat for just a moment before I say, "Yes, hi. The receptionist at my regular therapist's office said you might have an appointment for me? I mean, she said you guys—er, Dr. Kristen—sometimes kept afternoons if it was important. They can't see me here today and"—I stutter over my words— "I don't know. I'm hoping you can help me out?" It ends in a question. I almost resume my rambling, but the receptionist beats me to it.

"What is your name, sweetie?"

My back presses into the wall as I try to slow my heart rate. I can do this.

"Jennette Taylor, but I go by Jett."

"Hi, Jett. Our office is right off the square in Havenwood. What time can you be here?"

"I'm about an hour away, but I can head straight there from Atlanta."

"Okay, Jett. I'm putting you down for one thirty this afternoon. Does that work for you?"

I nod, unable to believe how unfazed she is by my unscheduled, spur of the moment appointment, before remembering she can't see me. "Oh, yes ma'am. I'll be there. Thank you."

"Not a problem at all, sweetie. We look forward to meeting you."

CHAPTER TWO

Noah

Four elevator banks. Fifteen cars. Thirty-five-hundred-pound capacity. Eight miles of multi-cable wires in the lobby panel alone. A mile of wiring per high-rise car. Half a mile per low-rise.

Numbers. Logic. Practical things.

That's me.

So, what is it about the girl from the entrapment call that has my head spinning? I should be focused on resetting the controls on car seven. Instead, her image keeps replaying in my head, a hint of lavender still consuming my senses.

I mean, yeah, she was gorgeous. Those toned legs and ass were the definition of perfection, showcased by her skin-tight jeans that came up high enough to hug her waist. An oversize sweatshirt tucked into her jeans concealed her upper body, but it was the lip she kept nibbling that had me completely entranced. I wanted that lip between my teeth more than I want a boss with a brain cell. My fingers flexed with the need to reach out and smooth it from her abusive grip just to pull it into mine. The intense focus on her lips almost—*almost*—distracted me enough to miss her emerald-green eyes.

What I wouldn't give to have a real conversation with her. To slip those loose tendrils of hair back behind her ear. To cradle her face in my hands as I trace my nose—

My thoughts scramble as my helper's voice crackles through the radio. "Hey, man, this door hates me or something. Can you come take a look?"

Rolling my eyes at Colt's lack of confidence in his own work, I slip the hand-held off my belt and answer. "It's basic wiring, bud. You should've learned it six months ago. They teach y'all anything these days?"

"Okay, jackass. Keep acting like that, and I'll tell Katie not to send you anymore apple pie cookies."

Huffing a laugh at the mention of Colt's wife and the most amazing cookies that—no joke—taste exactly like apple pie and trying to ignore his name-calling, I concede. "Come down to the lobby. I'll take a look after lunch."

Without permission, my mind drifts back to the girl. I didn't even get her name. Best believe I am kicking myself for that one.

I was working on a door issue when the power cut off and the chime sounded. Lucky for this girl, that car was in the same elevator bank. Otherwise, she would undoubtedly still be waiting for someone to show up an hour later. And judging by the messy brown hair that looked like fingers had constantly combed through it and the incessant fidgeting once she stepped through the doors, she would have had a panic attack before then.

As soon as she started rambling, I was a goner. The huskiness of her voice and dry sarcasm amid the panic sucked me right in.

"What're you camped out by the stairs for?"

"Shit." I jump, punching Colt in the arm for sneaking up on me. Although it probably wasn't much of a challenge.

He stares at me, a knowing glint in his eye. "She was a looker, huh? Waiting on her to come down?" He's not wrong.

"Mind your own damn business, man," I mumble as I stand, groaning when my left knee protests.

"You good?" he asks, staring at my leg like maybe it'll grow a mouth and talk.

"Don't ask stupid questions."

He doesn't need to know that turning thirty stole my ability to judge a jump onto a car top. It's just pain. It'll go away eventually.

Colt shrugs off my tone, weaving his way through the lobby.

"Hell, how do you know? You weren't even on the same floor."

"Passed her on the stairs. At least, I assume it was her. She was mumbling something about metal death traps and soot-covered men."

I chuckle, which is probably why Colt gives me a questioning look. I'm more the growly type. Something about the girl intrigues me, more than her looks. "Definitely her. I've never met someone who radiated innocence and chaos at the same time."

"Did you get her number?"

"I didn't even get her name."

"That sucks, man. But you know what else sucks? Working on an empty stomach. That cheesy, greasy goodness is calling my name."

It's pizza day. Nothing beats Fellini's Pizza. As we weave through the lunch crowd of the building, I catch a glimpse of the entrapment girl's profile. She must've slipped by while we were talking. Luck is not on my side, because the second I open my mouth to tell Colt I'll meet him at the restaurant around the corner, my phone rings, our boss's name flashing across the screen.

"You gotta be kidding me," I mutter before grabbing Colt's attention and pausing my steps while hitting the answer button.

"Yeah?" I grunt out. I'm not one to waste words, and nothing good ever comes from Ryan's calls.

"Hey. I need you and Colt to go to the shop and pick up some parts that some of the other guys need for tomorrow. Don't know if yours came in or not, but I need you to come sort them and see," Ryan says.

I bite back a groan as entrapment girl slips through the exit doors before I can take another step. Resigned to never learning more about her, I sigh. "Yep. We will be there a little after lunch," I grumble before hanging up.

A bunch of bullshit, if you ask me. Ryan is an asshat who doesn't know his foot from his ass when it comes to elevators. I can guarantee the parts he wants sorted are incorrect for the current project. He has no common sense.

I move toward the doors at a fast pace with the hope that this girl is still outside. Colt is quick to follow, but the mystery girl is already out of sight. Rubbing the back of my neck, I sigh again.

Damn it.

***

The worn wooden sign on the side of the road tells me I'm finally back home, but I don't need it. I could make this drive in my sleep. After traveling to the other side of Atlanta just to confirm that the wrong parts were ordered, I told Colt to go on home. The wiring issue can wait until next week. I'm more than ready for my three-day weekend of nothing.

I love this little town. The population is low, sitting at about twenty-five hundred, which is insane considering it borders city is known as "Hollywood of the South" due to all the movie and television productions that take place there. We don't have a Wal-Mart or a Publix. And the only drive-thru is the town's breakfast diner. The town square is home to most businesses and a few loft apartments that I own, thanks to some smart investing right out of high school.

I don't even have the key out of the doorknob or the door open all the way before I hear my Australian Shepherd yipping from her kennel. My keys clink on the counter as I drop them on my path to the room where her crate is. The moment her kennel door opens, Sadie launches into wiggling with what my sister refers to as tippy-tappies and wiggle-butts in excitement, whining and yipping her way between my legs.

"How's my Sadie Bear? D'you have a good day?" I ask as I scratch her neck and ears.

She yips again and takes off toward the back door. I let her out into the small, enclosed backyard and toss her tennis ball down the steps. It lands on the grass below, and I leave the door open for her as I start to clean up last night's dishes. I'd promised my best buddy Jace that I would come down to Riley's—his family-owned bar-slash-diner—to spend some time together since we'd both had hectic schedules lately. But before I can go out in public, I need to get some of this carbon dust and grease off me. My skin is coated in the shit, along with my lungs.

As I trudge back to the door to whistle for Sadie, my thoughts slip back to the girl from earlier. Or, woman, I guess. Though her entire presence screamed innocence. Chaotic, maybe. But there was something innately tender about her. I want to see her again. Hear her raspy voice. Get lost in those green eyes of hers as she nibbles on her lip.

I let out a deep sigh and shake my head to clear it of the images trying to evolve there and look at Sadie. "Pathetic, right?"

She sneezes, pawing at the floor.

"Yeah, I know. Get a grip, right?"

Sadie sneezes again before trotting over to her gray memory foam dog bed that takes up the entire far corner of the room. She has been through all the ups and downs of the last three years with me. My princess deserves all the spoiling.

"Behave yourself while I get cleaned up, yeah?"

She stares at me for a moment before dropping her head onto her paws, feigning sleep. Funny. As soon as I slip into the bathroom, she'll be running laps, getting into everything she isn't supposed to touch. Too nosy for her own good.

Sure enough, as soon as I start the shower faucet, I hear the speedy clicking of nails and sliding as she chases what is hopefully just a tennis ball around the living room. The last time I left her unsupervised, I lost a slipper and a pair of ear buds.

Shaking my head at the antics I know are underway, I slip out of my work clothes, making sure to toss them into the correct hamper. Can't have the oils and carbon dust mixing with my everyday wear. The hot water beats down on my sore muscles as I step under the shower spray and do everything possible to keep a certain brunette out of my thoughts. But every time my eyes close, the encounter consumes my senses. The smell of lavender, the softness of her hand in my calloused one, the vibrancy of her eyes. And that damn lip between her teeth.

I groan as my soaped-up hand glides lower, stroking my length firm and slow. Thoughts of pouty pink lips wrapping around me, those soft hands toying with whatever doesn't fit, have me on the edge faster than I'd like to admit.

Until Sadie barks once and scratches at the door, successfully destroying the best illusion I've had to date.

"You've gotta be kidding me," I mutter. I bang my forehead on the shower wall in frustration then reach for the handle and shut off the water.

Sadie barks again, which either means she needs to go outside or someone is at the door.

I better not have unexpected company. Or a pee puddle by the door.

Quickly wrapping a large fluffy towel around my waist, I open the bathroom door and look down the hall to find Sadie sitting at the front door. Damn. Someone is here. Also, don't hate on the fluffy towel. Men can prefer comfort over efficiency, too. I learned that the hard way nearly three years ago.

"Just a minute," I holler before running across the hall to my bedroom. I slip into the first pair of shorts I find and a gray V-neck before sprinting back to the front door. "Go lie down, girl."

It's none other than my tenant from the loft next door.

"Mrs. Grayson, is everything alright?"

"Oh, yes, dear. I just wanted to pass over the key. We decided to head out today instead of this weekend. The grandkids have a mid-winter break coming up, and we want to take them on an adventure." She holds out an envelope, which I assume has the key in it. "Thanks so much for being such a wonderful landlord and gentleman. Your mama should be proud of the boy she raised."

I take the proffered envelope and rub the back of my neck with the other hand. "I'd like to think she is, ma'am. Good luck transitioning to Florida weather."

"Looking forward to it, Noah." She turns and struts away, already hollering down the way to her husband. I close the front door and lean against it, looking at Sadie.

"Why couldn't it have been a cute brunette?"

Sadie groans, and I chuckle.

"Yeah, I know. Too much to ask for her to show up here." Oh, well. A guy can wish.

CHAPTER THREE

Jett

The drive to Havenwood isn't terrible. Luckily, most of the interstate traffic is on the east side.

I arrive in front of the tall, gray building right off the corner of the town's square. Okay, saying it's tall is a bit much. It's a three-story building. But I most definitely take the stairs to the third floor. I'll be staying far, far away from elevators for the foreseeable future.

The sweet lady from the phone—Willa—looks to only be in her mid-thirties, but she gives off some seriously strong nurturing vibes. Her small talk about the town's happenings helps keep my anxiety at bay as she leads me to a large office space with couches, beanbags, a desk, and a massive window that looks out toward River Haven Ranch. It isn't a fully functional ranch anymore—too much development nearby—but someone is out ground working what must be part of the newest training group of horses.

From what my brother Reece has told me, a new group of training and sale horses comes in about this time every year, and the two brothers who run it stay busy. I've only crossed paths with Drew and Declan a time or two, but I trust my brother that they are decent people. I doubt he'd still be working for them after five years if they weren't.

"Kristen is just taking a phone call and then she'll be right in with you," Willa says before stepping aside for me to pass through.

I just nod and give a weak "thanks" before sitting on the couch closest to the window. I slip out my phone, using the reading app to pick up where I left off in my latest romance read. The main character just found out her love interest was keeping his true motives from her, and she's struggling with the discovery.

I can relate.

I've made zero progress—reading the same passage...er, sentence multiple times—when a cute, petite lady waltzes in. She has to be about my age, with white-blonde hair and the palest-blue eyes I've ever seen. The smile on her lips lights up every part of her being. It's as if her happiness radiates throughout the room and is trying to sink into me through my pores. She approaches me with calculated steps, moving slowly as if closing in on a scared animal. Probably not an inaccurate comparison.

"Hi there. Jett, right? That's what you prefer?"

I nod, trying to find my words without throwing all my brain spam at her simultaneously. "Yes, please," I say, clearing my throat. "I hate my given name too much to use it on the regular." I mentally chastise myself for blabbing. This lady doesn't need my internal monologue.

"Nice to meet you, Jett. I'm Kristen. Not big on formalities around here," she says as she makes herself comfortable in the seat across from me. Once she's settled, she smiles again. "So, what's got you in here today?"

"I'm not really sure where to start," I admit, running my thumbnail up and down the opposite arm.

"How about we start with confirming your diagnoses, and we can go from there? I glanced over your file but want to make sure we're on the same page."

"Inattentive ADHD. Mild depressive episodes. Anxiety attacks. Just load me up with the neuro-spiciness, am I right?" Cringing, I do my best to make eye contact to convey my apology. "Sorry, I blab when I'm nervous, and today has been a day."

"There's no reason to apologize." She studies me for only a moment before asking, "Do you like dogs?"

I nod while picking at invisible lint on my jeans.

"Be right back," she says before hopping up and nearly skipping out the door. How in the world is she this giddy in the middle of a workday when she's listening to other people's problems all day?

Not two minutes later, she's back in the room with the absolute cutest red merle Australian Shepherd puppy on a leash. "This is Honor. She's a therapy dog in training. Sometimes it's easier for people to talk to her than it is to talk to me. Sometimes just giving your hands something to do like petting a dog can ease your anxiety as well." She leads Honor over to me. The purple harness vest with *Therapy Dog in Training* stitched on the sides nearly swallows the pup whole. Honor hops up next to me, and I scratch behind her ears, her back leg thumping a few times.

Kristen watches us for a moment before saying, "Why don't I hang back, and you tell her about whatever it is that's weighing so heavily on you." She unhooks the leash and walks over to her desk on the other side of the room before turning on some soft instrumental music.

I let the pup curl up in my lap, running my fingers through her fur. Her coat is almost down-like in texture. I feel for knots, sinking my fingers deep into the layers of hair, but find none. "You're such a cutie pie. But I bet you know that already."

She just looks at me expectantly, like she knows I am supposed to tell her my life's story. She can't be more than six months old, but there's an old soul looking out of those blue and brown eyes.

"Boys are icky. Stay away from them." That irritating feeling of pinpricks behind my eyes and the weight in my chest are back. I try, boy, do I try to keep the tears at bay. But I let my head fall forward, resting my forehead on the pup's side as a few tears escape. Honor curls tighter against me as if she knows I need the support.

"Relationships aren't for me, pup. If I haven't found a guy that can put up with all my sides by this point in life, I think it's safe to say that I won't. Maybe I'll just get twelve cats and be happy that way."

Honor tilts her head as if to call me on the lie.

"Yeah, you're probably right. I'll just get a couple puppies instead."

I go back to absentmindedly running my fingers through her coat. I don't know how much time passes, but I eventually lift my head, wiping the remaining wetness on the back of my hand. Kristen looks up from whatever she is working on at her computer, her glow still present.

"Sorry for having a breakdown in your office. I know you'd probably rather be anywhere else than in an appointment with someone who isn't actually a client. Especially one that isn't even talking to you."

She stands, coming back toward the couch but sitting far enough away so as not to invade the safety of the bubble-like area I've created. How she can sense that barrier, I don't know. I'm thankful, though, that she doesn't force me.

"There's nothing wrong with crying. If we kept it all bottled up, we'd make ourselves sick. This room is a safe space. As long as you aren't causing harm to yourself or someone else, anything goes in here. If that means you spend it receiving puppy snuggles, so be it."

I hum my understanding, fidgeting with my fingers after I've removed my hands from Honor. As soon as I recognize the nervous action, I return my hands to the red-and-white coat. My eyes stay focused on the dog, but I speak to Kristen.

"I found my boyfriend with his ding-dong in someone else's ditch."

I huff a laugh as I glance up in time to watch confusion flit across Dr. Flynn's face, but the corner of her lips rise in amusement. It is probably not my best analogy.

"I'd hate to interpret that incorrectly. Do you want to clarify what you mean?"

"Exactly how it sounds. He and his friend were getting it on whenever I wasn't around."

"And how are you handling it?"

"Oh, I'm not. I am effectively evading any and all emotions related to Joey. He can think I'm too much to handle all he likes." I sniffle, the slight burn in my throat and the tip of my nose giving away how close I am to tears. A little laugh escapes on a breath, although nothing about this is humorous. "Hell, if only that was the case. I'd love to be as strong as my words, but the truth is I'm barely holding it together."

"I'm sorry your ex couldn't recognize your attributes as the unique characteristics they are. How long ago was the breakup?" This lady truly looks interested in my sarcastic spiral. She's either a fantastic actress, or I've lucked up and found an empathetic therapist who gives a damn about her patients. I'm hoping it is the latter.

"About three weeks ago."

"And do you have a support system to help you move past it?"

"Technically I do, but I haven't told my brother or best friend much about what happened. Just that we split. They won't get it, why he left." My mind drifts off to the memory of that Tuesday afternoon and everything that was said. That day lives in a small box in the back of my mind, and the emotions are only allowed out to play when I am alone.

"It just happened, Jett. Maybe those feelings have always been there. I don't know. But one minute she was telling me about how she was hurting from her last breakup and the next we were

wrapped up in each other's arms. We were trying to find the right time to tell you."

"Before you played tonsil hockey in our living room would have been great." Ha, at least my sarcasm hasn't made a run for it yet. Then I really would be alone.

"Neither of us wanted to hurt you. You are." He pauses for a second, scrounging for words. "You are such a beautiful mix of delicacy and chaos and love, and I do care about you." He squeezes me, and I have to fight the instinct to sink into his hold. I hate that I still feel this much comfort in his arms.

"You're just not in love with me," I prompt, knowing I'm right.

The loss of his body heat as he takes a step back is almost too much, but as he turns me to face him and wipes away a tear I didn't know I'd shed, he cups my cheek. Glassy eyes look back at my own.

"I know it was wrong to keep it from you—"

"You should have told me when you realized things had changed."

"I should have told you."

I take a steadying breath, already compartmentalizing the situation. I'll break down over this later. Right now, I want answers more than I want to wallow. "Why?"

He looks away as he says, "As much as I love who you are, it's also...a lot to handle. I was drowning trying to keep up with your ever-changing hobbies, trying to keep this place organized, trying to keep both of us pleased in the bedroom when you were rarely ever truly there."

When I slip out of the memory, Kristen is waiting patiently as she has the entirety of this session. I give her a rundown of the day of our breakup without much inflection in my tone.

"It sounds like Joey was struggling with some of his own worries and didn't know how to direct and discuss those thoughts and feelings. But you have every right to feel those heavy thoughts toward your relationship. Aside from what you've already shared, how is this situation affecting your day-to-day living?"

The trembling of my hands doesn't stop as I wipe my eyes again, expecting to feel tears on my face but finding it dry. I breath in a lungful of air and hold it for a few counts before letting it out.

"I don't know what I'm doing," I admit my fears with a defeated shrug. "I've lost my drive. My routine is shot. I can't sleep in the bed, because it was our bed even when it didn't feel like our bed, so I've been curling up in the oversize chair in the office room. I don't know how to push past it. I don't want him to come back—I know we were done and that this was just the final nail in the coffin—but I also want the security of a partner.

"And then on top of that, I lost the job I've been absolutely rocking for the last eight years. Now, I'm dipping my toes in the freelancing waters, and organizing my life needs to be a priority, but I really just want to curl into a ball and not come out for a week or six. Or if I could just blink and have this be a nasty nightmare."

By the time my monologue is complete, I've sunk even deeper into the cushions of the couch, seeking comfort from the dog pressed to my side.

Dr. Kristen's stare holds a multitude of emotions but remains professional at the same time. "How have your ADHD symptoms been, Jett? Medications working?" she asks before looking down at her notepad then back at me. "Excessive stimming?"

I hum in confirmation. "More than I was before Christmas."

"And what about your depression? I'm assuming that's why you wanted to meet today."

I nod, a small whimper escaping from my lips. "Sorry." I clear my throat.

"Our feelings are meant to be felt and expressed. Never apologize for that."

The thought spiral starts before I can shift to a new topic: catching Joey and Ella together, Joey's parting words, my boss's impersonal dismissal after I put my heart into my job, the fear of proving everyone right.

A tear finally leaks past my defenses.

Honor nudges my hand with her nose, and I realize that at some point I stopped running my fingers through her coat to pick at my jeans again.

"If I say it out loud, it makes all of this real," I finally whisper.

"We can't face our demons if we let them stay burrowed deep inside us."

Unlovable. Unworthy.

Lazy. No drive. No determination.

Negatives I've heard throughout my life play through my mind, but I do my best to silence them.

Instead, I say, "Right now, everything is utterly out of control and my chest feels so heavy that I can barely breathe most days. It's constant anxiety attacks and forcing myself out of bed. I spent the last week feeling numb, praying that things would magically go back to normal."

"It sounds like you've had a lot of heavy life events thrown your way all at once. Why don't we try working through one at a time to see what we can come up with, yeah?"

Another shaky breath. Another brush of my fingers through Honor's coat as we sift through the emotions I've bottled up for too many weeks. "It's not even the loss of my relationship, you know? I knew we were done long before finding him compromised, but the betrayal of a two-year commitment followed by everything else is crushing me."

As I explain that the loss of my position at a local press is what tipped the scales, Kristen shifts the conversation.

"What do you think moving forward looks like for you? I'd like to help you put a plan in motion to find your footing."

Rubbing a hand over my face, the faint smell of puppy tickling my nose, I groan as I realize all the tasks that I've abandoned recently. "I need to find somewhere to move. My name was on the lease, but I've kind of already decided that reliving what I saw every time I walk through the front door is more than I want to handle." My voice trembles as I add, "I need a fresh start, but that seems like the hardest thing in the world right now."

"You don't need all the answers right this minute. Take some time to think about what you want your future to look like without anyone else's influence. Where you live, what dreams you chase, and who you chase those dreams with are all decisions for you to make. No one else. Just think on it, and we can discuss it if or when you are ready."

I nod, and Honor licks my tearstained cheek before hopping off the couch.

"I am always around if you ever want to chat. Scheduled or not. In office or out. Don't hesitate to reach out, okay?" Kristen hands me a sticky note with what looks to be her cell number.

"I hate to ask since you've already done so much, but any chance you know of open rentals?"

"Have you been to Riley's Bar and Grill? There's a bulletin board right inside the door where citizens post any town knowledge. You might find something there."

Jokingly, I ask, "What about sexy elevator mechanics?"

The amusement on Kristen's face is palpable, like she knows a secret I don't. "We have one of those around here. Though I don't know if *I* consider him sexy. My husband is a little too alpha for me to admit something like that."

"Mmm, a growly man. Good for you."

The knowing smile she shares lets me know I'm correct.

"Check out the board at Riley's. If nothing is listed, ask the owner. His buddy owns most of the rental properties in this town."

As she hooks the leash back to Honor's harness and I walk toward the door, Kristen calls my name. I turn to look at her, and she grins. "If you're into grumbly men, that not-sexy elevator mechanic usually hangs around Jace Riley. Just in case." She winks.

My cheeks flame as I thank her, clutching her phone number in my fist. I want to be as confident as Kristen Wilson-Flynn when I grow up.

CHAPTER FOUR

Jett

"I think I might move here," I blurt, interrupting Reece's spiel about his current gig as a ranch hand.

His head jerks in my direction, hand pausing its stirring. Big brother is making chicken Alfredo, one of the best comfort foods ever created. Also, proof that he's still trying to baby me.

"I'm sorry. I could have sworn you just interrupted my fascinating story about Havoc and his hay bale shenanigans to tell me you're moving?"

Nodding eagerly, I snatch a piece of shredded chicken from his cutting board. "Well, not yet, obviously. I haven't found a place to live yet. I just decided on it today. Living near you can't be too bad, and it makes getting here easier than driving from the other side of Covington. Hey, isn't Havoc the horse that broke your boss? Is he still broken?"

Reece chuckles while rubbing a hand over his face like I exhaust him.

Fun fact, I do.

"Yeah, Jett. Drew is still broken, but I don't think he'd appreciate you phrasing it like that." He pauses, looking off thoughtfully. "Though I think it's more than just his shoulder, honestly. He's seemed off, like he's not fully there on the days he comes out to supervise." Then he waves his sauce-covered spatula at me. "Stop changing the subject, missy. Moving. Since when? Where are you thinking?"

"Since my rent is up in three weeks—"

"Damn it, Jett. You have to stop doing that with your living arrangements," he interrupts.

My words keep rolling without pause, ignoring the brother bear act. "—and I don't want to stay in the same house that Joey and I shared anymore, since he left me for someone else. You're here. My new therapist is here. She suggested it actually. Well, sort of. Maybe not *suggested* as much as just asked if I was going to? Anyway, I met with her for the first time, like, three hours ago. And then McKenna is only fifteen minutes away. It's perfect."

"Hold on. Go back. What the hell, Jennette? You said he left. Not that it was because of another person."

Oops. I forgot I haven't shared that little turd nugget about Joey yet, but Reece isn't done. I woke brother bear. He's such a happy-go-lucky individual until I cause him stress.

"And did you say your *new* therapist? And honestly, why haven't you mentioned that your lease was almost up? I would've helped you secure a place."

I shrug, vaguely grasping the fact I've once again procrastinated in an area I most definitely shouldn't. Although it wouldn't be the first time if I end up in my brother's guest room for something similar. I could find a little place like this. Two-bedroom, single bath, open floor plan. It could be cute. Well, until the doom piles eventually take over the corners of the living space.

"Jett. Focus," Reece says, tapping the counter in front of me. Irritation is brewing in his eyes, but he's doing his best to keep his cool. I'm a pro at pulling out the angry side of him. It seems to be reserved for me and McKenna. Our dad always jokes that the eleven months separating me and Reece in age wasn't enough time for our mom to refill the optimism jar, but quite honestly, I don't think my brother is too optimistic when it comes to me surviving on my own.

"Right, so there was this incident today where I got stuck in an elevator and missed my appointment and they couldn't reschedule, but I needed to have an appointment today because I was fixating, right? They gave me a number for the therapist here in Havenwood, and I really like her and I don't have to drive on the interstate to get to an appointment."

"Jennette Marie Taylor, what in the world?"

"I know, right?" I say while grinning, winded from my continuous spout of words. "And there was this guy—the elevator mechanic—who saved me. He was a little growly, but he talked me through everything and I didn't have an anxiety attack." My shoulders relax on a sigh, the tension from the day slowly seeping away. Until I focus on Reece and recognize the look on his face.

"Why the hell didn't you tell me about Joey?"

"I did."

"No, you said you guys broke up. Not that he left you for someone else. So, he was cheating?" The anger coming off him is palpable. He thought Joey and I were planning our forever. Everyone did.

Rolling my eyes at Reece, I say, "So you could end up in jail for assault? No thanks. And I don't want to talk about him. I just want him to disappear from my memories while I wait for a fictional knight in shining armor to sweep me off my feet. One who treats me like a princess and brings his own crazy to the relationship. Just like you and Dad always said I deserved."

Reece shakes his head at me as he mixes in the last ingredients—basil butter, at least a pound of mozzarella, and cream cheese—into the gigantic pot on the stove. Once he is satisfied with the consistency of the Alfredo sauce, he turns off the burner and approaches me from around the corner of the bar-style counter, sliding his phone in front of me. I look questioningly at it then stare back at him, my eyebrows furrowed. Before I can ask, he nods toward the calendar on the fridge.

"Mom has already tried to call. Twice. Call her back."

A groan works its way up my throat. I do not want to tune in to this week's disappointment session. "Can't you just pretend I'm sick or something?"

He gives me a pointed look and taps the phone's screen. Pouting with an audible sigh, I unlock the screen and hit the contact for our mother. Silently, I beg for her not to answer. For her to be too busy with her perfect little family.

Am I bitter that she and our dad split during my junior year of high school, Reece's senior? Not really. Turns out they had only stayed married out of convenience and friendship—and their children—but our mom had fallen in love with her assistant. She and Luke married not long after she left us. Reece and I now have two little sisters that we—well, I—only see a few times each year. My big-hearted brother sees them regularly.

So, no. I'm not bitter about the divorce.

My frustration comes from our mom's inability to understand me.

She tried her best, but even now she usually hands off any Jennette issues to our dad or Reece.

For the last three years, Reece and I have had standing calls on Thursday evenings. Just like when we were kids, Mama expects me to engage in the conversation and share everything happening in my life. And just like when we were kids, I always disappoint her.

Pressure on my forearm brings my attention back around as Reece squeezes it. "Hi, Mama. Yeah. We're both here," he says while giving me a gentle second nudge, and I realize I must have missed her answering the call.

"My oldest babies. How are y'all this week? What's new?"

Reece eyes me, waiting for me to expose who knows what. I widen my eyes at him in innocence and shrug. I do not feel like explaining myself to a voice on a speaker. What's the point if I can't stay focused on the conversation at hand?

"Not much new going on at the farm. No new love interests for you to interrogate. Jett, how 'bout you? Wanna tell mom what's new with you?"

If eyes could set people on fire, my brother would be roasting right now.

"Fill me in, Jett. I'm still waiting for the girls to come out of dance practice, so give me all the details you can muster."

My eyes close, as if not seeing my surroundings will somehow erase this moment from time.

"Nothing really, Mama. Just been spending some time out here with Reece and getting ready to devour some Alfredo, but overall life's a peach."

The beat of total silence and Reece rubbing the back of his neck clues me in to my biggest mistake of the evening.

"Jennette, honey," Mama prods gently, like she is coddling a toddler. "Reece only makes that dish when you're having a rough go. What's happened?"

I groan audibly, looking at Reece for help.

"Don't try that just because I can't see you, Jett. You are too old to let your brother do the talking for you. What is going on that has your brother stressed enough to cook chicken Alfredo?" Of course, the woman who raised us knows when I try to deflect situations to my brother even when she can't see us.

My knee bounces of its own free will. Just like when I lived under her roof, my muscles draw tight, tension building between my shoulder blades. The flat-out refusal to answer her question is on the tip of my tongue, but my lungs squeeze a breath out.

I'm trying to become a better version of me. A stronger version. One that doesn't cower from conversations with people who love her.

"Joey left. I got stuck in an elevator, I changed therapists, and I'm moving. Sorry. Gotta go. Love you, Mom." Before

Reece can sense my plan, I slam my thumb against the end button, cutting off the call and staring at the device on the counter while my breathing turns ragged.

I can't take in enough oxygen. The familiar sting of tears sits behind my eyes, but I shut it down. I refuse to shed one more tear over this nightmare of a month. And maybe it wasn't a great first try at being strong, but it's more than I have done in recent months.

Reece tries to wrap a comforting arm around my shoulders, but I push back. I can't handle being touched right now. Even the material of my favorite sweatshirt feels like too much contact, the fibers scratching against my skin.

"I'm going for a walk. Please don't follow." I push away from the counter and rush to the entryway, grabbing my lined raincoat on the way. The rain stopped a few hours ago, but this time of year, you just never can quite trust the weatherman in Georgia.

I don't have a destination in mind, since I've never taken the time to explore Havenwood. Reece moved here a few years ago, but the only thing we ever do when I come to visit is stay in at his house. On the rare occasion that I travel anywhere here, I find myself at the little bar and diner owned by Jace Riley. I'll add it to my to-do list to explore the town so many people love.

And that's the thing. Loving this town is a requirement for living here. Outsiders know almost nothing about it. It's like stepping into a small-town romance novel, complete with a bar and grill, coffee shop, bed-and-breakfast, and a town square where constant community activities take place. Old cattle properties make up the outer border of the town, and the Flynn family ranch—River Haven Ranch—makes up the south part of town.

I wander around the square, taking in the leftover Christmas decorations—twinkling lights in the trees and wreaths on the lampposts—all around me as my mind runs through too many thoughts and scenarios for me to fully grasp any of them.

The beauty of the small-town perfection isn't enough to keep me in the here and now. My mind is stuck on replay. I walked away from Reece and Mama. Again. Just like I did with Joey. Just like I always do when I get overwhelmed.

Against better judgment, I make my way to Riley's. I slip through the door unnoticed and take a seat at the far end of the bar. My head falls into my hands while I try to drown out the multiple voices and trains of thought flitting through my mind. Maybe a few shots of whiskey will quiet things for me. Lord knows it's been a hell of a day.

CHAPTER FIVE

Noah

Thursday nights are meant to be relaxing.

I work four tens, which means Friday kicks off my weekend. The list of to-dos this weekend is extensive, and I should get a head start, but instead I'm on the sidewalk outside of Riley's.

I promised my buddy Jace I'd come into the bar tonight. His family has owned it for generations, and when his dad decided not to run it anymore, Jace took over. He turned it into the most active evening hangout spot in our little town. It serves as a studying location, a dinner and date spot, and a hang-and-drink kind of place.

As I slip through the door, I register the soothing tones of Johnny Cash playing through the speakers. I pause at the giant bulletin board that has always been a catch-all of sorts to pin a *Rental Available* card to it.

Weaving through the tables, I make my way to the bar stools at the back. Jace smiles when he sees me. The dude is six-four and built like a linebacker. The teddy bear also cried at the end of *Homeward Bound*. I met him my first day in Havenwood shortly after settling in at my aunt's house. The move had been unexpected, but at fifteen, I was already battling demons that couldn't be slayed if I stayed in Steele Valley.

To say he'd intimidated me would be an understatement. He walked up to me without reason and started talking about root beer floats and asking if I wanted to get one, too. I was more of a keep-to-myself kind of guy, but Jace and his best friend Drew always included me in every situation.

"Dude, what's got you all smiley and shit? You bang a chick in one of your elevators today or something?" He laughs at his own joke, knowing I'm not one to mess around with random women. Funny, though, how close he is to what I wish had happened.

"What're you talking about, man?"

"You haven't quit smiling since you sat down. It's weird. You're usually mister grump and misery."

"Rude."

"True." He sets to pouring me a rum and Coke before sliding over a paper coaster and placing the glass on top of it.

I chuckle to myself, wiping a hand over my face to sober my voice. "Had an entrapment during that band of storms this morning. There was a woman in it, alone. Probably a few years younger than me."

Jace's eyes light with amusement at the realization that his theory at least holds some merit.

"Noah, man. I was kidding about shacking up. Tell me you didn't."

I full on belly laugh at that. "No, Jace. I did not *shack up* with the girl I rescued. But I am still kicking myself for not getting her name. She looked a little familiar, but I know I'd have remembered this one."

"Let me guess. Brunette. Green eyes. An ass and some sass."

"Are you serious right now, bud?"

"You have a type, *bud*." He grins, nodding over my shoulder at someone.

I realize a moment later that it is the third to our friend group when Jace yells out a greeting.

"Yo, Drew. Green-eyed beauty with brown hair and an ass. Who's gettin' her?"

Drew slides onto the stool next to me, a twitch of his lip the only sign of humor. "Definitely not yours, Jacey-Boy."

Jace jokingly whips his towel at Drew, but his eyes hold a hint of worry like they usually do these days. Something happened to Drew a few months back, but none of us know what. Drew went out of town with his brother and came back closed off. Neither brother would spill, but the rift in their relationship is still prominent. Things have continued to worsen since Drew's accident shortly after their return. He fractured his back and collarbone and has a shit ton of shoulder damage.

A look at my face has Jace backtracking. "You know I'm just pullin' your leg, right, Noah?"

I wave him off. "No worries, man."

The teasing is nice after so many days, months, years of not taking an interest in anyone. I should run the other way from any thoughts of another relationship. I couldn't protect anyone three years ago, and nothing has changed.

Jace studies me for a moment longer before looking back at Drew. "You quit using your braces, now?" he asks immediately after noticing the black straps are absent.

Drew blows off both the question and the concern, asking, "Where's your twin?"

Jace nods toward the back. "Kelsey is doing inventory, so you're shit outta luck, bud. She's already been told not to pour you anything but water tonight." Jace slides a can of soda over to him. "Jack and Coke, hold the Jack."

Drew rolls his eyes but doesn't fight the drink choice. "You think you're cute, huh?"

Jace offers a cheeky grin. "The ladies seem to think so."

I almost comment on the fact that Jace has cut Drew off before he's even started, but my words falter as movement at the far end of the bar catches my eye. I swat my hand excitedly at Jace's arm and whisper harshly, "That's her, man. That's the girl from my entrapment call."

How lucky could I be that she'd show up here, of all places? This town doesn't get visitors, so what's she doing here? Drew looks confused, and I can't blame the guy; he missed that part of the conversation.

"Shit," Jace mutters before he saunters to the other side of the bar, and I can hear the girl's soft voice.

"Double shot of Red Stag, please." Leggings hug her ass and thighs, and the same sweatshirt from that morning sits lopsided on her shoulders. A twisted mess of a braid hangs over her shoulder. The low lighting of the bar does nothing to hide her tear-streaked cheeks, and the sight of those tracks does strange things to my heart that I don't want to acknowledge.

Because Jace is right.

I am not the type of guy to hook up with a random girl. I'd always prided myself on being a relationship guy, but I swore those off a few years ago after tragedy struck our little town. It's just me and Sadie these days. She is the only girl I need in my life. Loyal to a fault and always up for snuggles without the baggage.

But something about this girl—natural beauty, not trying to impress anyone—has been tugging at my heartstrings since our encounter.

Jace pours the double shot she requested without question, and something about my mystery girl shooting her shot without so much as a wince before putting the glass in front of Jace, saying, "another," and repeating the process cuts through some more of the barbed wire around the ticker in my chest. When she tries for a third shot, Jace shakes his head.

Good. Otherwise, I would have found myself overstepping on a stranger's drinking habits.

"Food first. Last time you came in, you swore you had eaten then nearly passed out on my bar." He drops his voice so I can't hear what he says next, but his eyes cut to me.

I vaguely register Drew's arm reaching over to the back side of the bar and grabbing the discarded whiskey bottle, pouring some directly into his Coke can, and returning the bottle. I'll try to remember to question Jace later. Before I can convince myself of what a terrible idea it might be, I stand and make my way over.

"You followin' me now?" I ask as I slip onto the barstool next to her.

She jumps, startled. Her wide eyes trail up to my face slowly. When she finally makes eye contact, surprise lights her face and a touch of a smile graces her lips, but both are gone in a flash, washed out by the red rimming her eyes.

"I guess this makes you the sexy elevator man my new therapist told me about."

I chuckle. "Don't think I want to know why you and Drew's sister-in-law were talking about me." Before I can stop myself, I reach up to wipe away some of the remaining dampness left by her tears. "Sexy, huh?"

She lets out a short laugh at that, but the humor doesn't reach her eyes. "Wasn't expecting it to be *my* elevator man when I jokingly asked if there were any around here."

I shake my head, but I can't keep the sheer satisfaction at her innocent claim from affecting me. "*Your* elevator man, huh? *And* you think I'm sexy. My ego thanks you for that boost."

That earns me a slightly more noticeable grin, but she tucks her chin and snags a fry from the basket Jace set in front of her.

"Noah," I introduce before fighting the urge to smack myself in the face.

She knows your name, dumbass.

Still, I hold my hand out to her. She hesitates for a second before dusting salt from her fingers and placing her hand in mine. Such tiny, soft hands.

"Jett."

"That's different."

"I'm different."

That you are, I think.

Before I can say more, Jace interrupts. His eyes burn a hole into mine as he says, "You eating this here, Jett, or you takin' it back to Reece's house?"

She blows a piece of hair that has loosed itself from her braid and sighs heavily. "Brother bear already called looking for me?"

"Yep," Jace says, popping the P.

"Guess I'm heading back there, then. Can you pack it up for me, please?"

I'm not used to the heavy feeling of disappointment pressing down on me simply because someone is leaving. I look out the door and curse to myself as I realize how late it's gotten. "You good to drive there? It's getting dark out, and I just watched you down two doubles like they were nothing."

"My brother's place is right down the road. It's lighted all the way there, and I never even have to step off the sidewalk."

Try as I might, I can't keep the exasperation out of my voice. "You're walking home? It's forty degrees out and the sun'll be down before you get off Main Street."

"What's the matter, elevator man? Worried you won't get to see me again?"

A playful look creeps into her eyes, drawing me in. I do not want this girl to walk out of here. Not because the people of Havenwood aren't trustworthy—this town is built around family—but because I know how quickly things can go from safe to tragic when the sun goes down.

And maybe she is right. What if I don't see her again?

I refuse to dig deeper into that thought.

"Let me walk you home?" I ask, seeing the steely determination within her. The playfulness is still there, but something else sits on the edge.

"I don't even know your last name. How could I possibly trust that you aren't trying to lure me away to a remote location to have your way with me before offing me and positioning my body to fill some crazed murder fantasy of yours?"

A chuckle rumbles through my chest, even with the tension I feel at the thought of her walking out of this bar alone. "You definitely have an active imagination, chaos."

Although, part of her statement is spot on. I'd love to lure her away to fulfill a different type of fantasy if I wasn't more worried about her on the sidewalk at dusk.

"I appreciate the concern for my safety, Noah. It's been a pleasure running into you, and while you are a fine specimen to behold, I'll let you in on a little secret. I am a total shit show and not worth your time. Hot mess central right here."

She stands from her stool, hands gesturing to herself as Jace appears with the bagged food and a comment about her brother waiting out front for her. Her fists clench for a moment before she lets out another heavy sigh, like the weight of the world is pressing down around her.

Her eyes hold gallons of pain in this moment, and stress lines marring her beautiful face. Gone is the girl who was dishing out novel-worthy plot lines moments ago. In her place is a crumbling shell of the spirited spitfire from the elevator. The urge to touch her, to comfort her, is almost too much.

What the hell is going on with me?

"Let me walk you out, Jett," I offer, removing the bag from her hand and offering her my other arm.

After a moment's hesitation, she takes it.

We walk in silence to a silver Ford pickup where Reece Taylor is waiting in the driver's seat. I try—and fail—to contain my groan. Of course, Reece is her brother. That's what Jace's looks were about.

Reece Taylor hates me. I don't know what I did to him. I do know I am an ass most of the time, but people usually deserve it. I've barely spoken to Reece in however many years he has been here, but the glare he's shooting me right now tells a different story. I tuned out Jace's warning glance when he'd mentioned Reece by name, but now it's all too real.

"Jett, as in Jennette Taylor?"

She glances at me, confusion in her eyes. "The one and only disappointment of my mother's loins. What of it?"

"Nothing, just trying to calculate how long I have before your brother tries to separate me from my favorite body parts."

That lip twitch comes and goes so fast that I wonder if I imagine it. "He's harmless, unless you're me."

"He hates me." Even I can hear how pathetic I sound.

"What are you, twelve?" The lip twitch is more prominent this time. "And don't worry. He strongly dislikes me most days, too."

"Not twelve, just cautious. Your brother is not someone to mess with. I've seen the livestock he wrangles."

"Good thing you're not wasting your time with me then, huh?"

I shake my head. "You hang around here long enough, and I bet I can change your mind. I have a feeling you are more than worth my time."

"Goodbye, Noah."

When I slip back into the bar, Jace and Drew are in a heated whisper-yell match. By the time I am close enough, all I can hear is what sounds a lot like a threat from Jace.

"—telling Declan if you don't. This ain't somethin' you can handle on your own, brother."

The knuckles of Drew's good hand are white with the grip he has on the bar top. I hesitate as Jace catches my eye. Drew's are glued to the wall past Jace's shoulder.

"Everything okay?" I ask, not at all sure what I just stepped in.

Drew stands, favoring his left side. The grimace makes even me hurt, and I sling around elevator equipment for a living. My joints are as bad as an eighty-year-old.

"Nothin' to worry about," Drew says as he walks stiffly to the door.

I watch him for a moment before looking back at Jace. There's one giant, polka-dotted elephant in here, and the last thing I want to do is get into a deep conversation after the day I've had, but I still voice my concern. "He okay?"

Jace shakes his head but doesn't make eye contact. "He says the pain's still killin' him. If he's still poppin' those pain pills, I'm not gonna be responsible for him dousing his innards with alcohol. Drinkin's what got him in this mess to begin with."

I shoot a sympathetic glance his way. "He's always made his own choices, Jace. Alcohol just happens to be one of the less enjoyable ones."

He levels a glare at me, although I know it isn't actually *at* me. "This is where he got drunk before he stumbled to the barn, jumped on an unbroke colt, and ended up underneath it. My best friend nearly died. He's not touching the alcohol in this place for a long damn time."

I rub the back of my neck, debating if I should hold back on outing Drew but feeling the weight in Jace's words. How it is clearly weighing on his conscience. Jace stands a little straighter, intimidating me without saying a word. I've retaken my seat, looking guilty.

Wincing, I point at the red soda can still on the bar. "When you were taking Jett's drink order, he topped off his Coke with whiskey."

Jace glances at the can then back at me as he lifts it to his nose, takes a whiff, and curses. "Damn him."

I just nod, not sure what to do with the knowledge he's dropped on me. Jace sighs, shaking his head before turning to assist another patron a few seats down. When he returns, I can tell he's switched gears on me. It's not uncommon. I think it comes with being a bar owner and always having to adjust and shift conversation depending on which patron he is speaking with.

"So, Jett, huh?"

Shaking my head, I say, "You couldn't have warned me? Like *really* warned me she was Reece Taylor's little sister?"

He chuckles. "Honestly, I can't believe you didn't know it was her. She comes into town a few times a month. Usually has a rough night somewhere in there and ends up here. Reece checks here first before sending out the hounds. Man, you're screwed."

Groaning, I drop forward onto the bar. "It's not funny, man. That guy hates me, and I know it can't be anything I did."

Jace full on belly laughs. "Because you're such a lovable guy, right? Are you tellin' me you really don't know why he hates you?"

"No, I've done nothing to him. I swear. I've never even had a reason to speak more than a few words to him."

He stares, clearly not believing me. "Dude, your brother slept with his fiancée. How do you not know this?"

Well, shit.

CHAPTER SIX

Jett

Reece is quiet on the short drive back to his house.

My anxiety builds as he puts the truck in park, the four shots of liquor I had trying to make themselves known. Thankfully, Jace didn't let me keep drinking. He learned his lesson the first time I stepped foot in Riley's Bar and Grill. I hurled all over the freshly polished bar top.

"I know you're hurting, sis, but you can't keep running from the people who want what's best for you." Reece's voice is gravelly with emotion. Emotion I try to lock in the darkest corners of my brain.

Like talking to our mom.

Or discussing failed relationships.

Or failed jobs.

Or life in general.

By the time I've registered his heavy sigh, he has already opened the truck door and stepped out. I groan. I'd been stuck in my head again and missed who knows what. I jump out of the truck and catch up to my brother.

"What did you say after the thing about running?"

"Nothing, Jett," he mumbles, an air of frustration pouring off of him.

My stomach drops at the dismissal. Or is that the liquor again? On that note, I'm not sure the last time I ate except for the handful of fries.

"I'm sorry I tuned you out. What did you say?"

He shakes his head, the irritation that only I can trigger obvious in his posture and tone. "Don't worry about it. Guest room has clean sheets. I already hid your keys, so no bright ideas about going home tonight. Guess I shouldn't have cooked the Alfredo after all, since apparently Jace feeds you better," he grumbles, motioning toward the takeout bag.

My shoulders sag, but before I can apologize, he stops me, palms raised by his stomach and voice dropping to a soothing tone.

"It's okay, sis. It'll heat fine tomorrow. Get some sleep. We can talk in the morning." With that, he turns and walks to his room on the other side of the house.

I wait as his footsteps fade and the door to his room clicks shut before putting the food from the bar away and sitting in the armchair closest to the kitchen.

I shouldn't let it get to me. Irritating Reece is at minimum a weekly occurrence; twenty-seven years hasn't changed anything. But something about tonight has those tightly guarded emotions leaking through the cracks.

My mind spins, so many thoughts trying to take over, but none of them make enough of an impression to stick.

***

The buzz of something vibrating across the floor wakes me from a deep sleep. It takes a few minutes for me to realize it is my phone. Groaning, I stretch out the kinks in my spine. I moved to the guest room around midnight, but the mattress is too firm for comfort. Sleep didn't find me until about two hours ago. Maybe I should convince Reece to get one of those eggcrate mattress toppers for when he has people over.

I snatch my phone off the floor when it vibrates again and glance at the screen, seeing three missed calls and two texts from my best friend.

McKenna: Girl, where are you?

McKenna: Went by the house but your car was gone.

Jett: At Reece's

McKenna: Nevermind.

Jett: Can you drive down?

Jett: The bar right on the square. 12:30?

McKenna: See you then. ILY.

The smell of coffee draws me out of my room; Reece must have started a pot while I was texting McKenna. I stand and make my way into the kitchen, set on apologizing for last night. He's pouring creamer into a large coffee cup but looks up as I slide onto the stool at the breakfast bar.

"I'm sorry." My voice shakes, almost breaking.

"I know telling you not to worry about it is pointless, because you'll just worry more, but I mean it. It's no big deal. There's just a lot going on for both of us right now, emotions were high, and seeing you with Noah Slater threw me."

"He hinted that you aren't his biggest fan." My eyebrows raise, curiosity getting the best of me as I fix my own mug. Mostly creamer and sugar.

Reese cuts his eyes at me over the rim of his mug. "I know it's pointless to tell you what to do—I learned that lesson years ago—but stay away from Noah. Those elevator guys are all assholes."

I choke on a laugh, thankful I haven't taken a sip of the coffee in my hands yet. "I'm sorry, what?"

His lip twitches. "It's true."

"How would you even know that? How many elevator guys do you actually know?"

He shakes his head, fighting silent laughter. "Okay, I only know Noah and one other."

It's my turn to shake my head as he continues.

"But I've heard enough to know they are a different breed."

"Are you sure you aren't just saying that because Dad used to always say it about every trade other than electrical?"

At that, a real laugh finally rolls through my brother. Our dad was an electrician for nearly thirty years before retiring early. We heard the beef between union trades the entirety of our childhood.

"Okay, maybe his words contributed to my opinion. Slightly."

"I still don't understand your warning, though. Noah is just the guy that saved me from the stuck elevator. We just happened to run into each other. It's not like—"

"Hold up, what?"

"What, what?" I snap, irritated by the interruption.

"Noah was the mechanic?"

I cock a brow at him, waiting on him to catch up with my thoughts.

"I'll never understand how your brain works."

"Join the club. I've lived twenty-seven years with it and still haven't figured out how it works. Anyway, I already told him I wasn't interested or worth his time, so no need for brother bear to come out and eat anyone. But McKenna is meeting me for lunch at Riley's, and you should join us."

Reece's eyes harden. "I think I'll pass."

"I've had one of the worst months of my life and want my brother and my best friend to eat lunch with me. Can you guys pretend to get along for an hour or two to make that happen?" I pout. For a second, I think my brother will give an honest answer for once, but then a sarcastic grin lights his face.

"Because she hogs you, and I want you all to myself."

"Ha ha ha. You are absolutely hilarious."

When he says nothing more, I add, "I would really like to only admit to everything that has been going on once. Can you please just act like civilized human beings for one lunch?"

Reece groans. I don't know what happened between them, but I hate that my two favorite people cannot stand to be in the same room as each other ninety-eight percent of the time.

I push away from the counter and head to the guest room's connected bathroom to shower and get ready. "Riley's at twelve thirty. It'd be really cool if you joined us."

After a quick wash of the hair, I slip into some of my softest sweatpants and a bookish tee. It's of a fictional hockey team from a book series, and I could not help myself when I saw it. I forego socks and slip my bare feet into my Sketchers. Instead of brushing and drying my hair, I secure it in a messy bun as exhaustion makes its existence known. And no, this is not some cutesy messy bun. This is an *I'm tired and my hair is long so let us please get it out of the way without cutting it off* messy bun. It's typically my go-to hair style.

As I slip out of the guest room, I hear the water turn on across the hall.

Success. Brother is going to go after all.

***

Reece and I sit in tense silence in a booth at the back of Riley's dining area.

My knee is bouncing so uncontrollably that I'm sure a hole is about to open under us from the vibrations. Reece keeps an eye on me as he scrolls through his phone. McKenna nearly skips through the tables, but then her eyes land on my brother and her steps falter briefly. She shoots daggers at me, and I send her serious *please don't hate me* vibes. Her steps resume, but her entire aura has shifted to something much less enthusiastic as she slips into the spot next to me, across from Reece.

"Now that your keeper is here, can we get on with it?" Reece grunts without glancing away from his screen.

My teeth dig into the inside of my cheek at the dig at McKenna, but it hurts me, too. My hand comes up to rub at my temple, brushing a stray hair that escaped the nest on top of my head.

McKenna nudges my leg under the table but looks at Reece and says, "I'm not her keeper, and you know it. Your sister is a big girl. Treat her as such."

"I know she is."

"Then watch what you say and how it affects those around you."

My brother's jaw clenches as he looks away for a minute then raises a hand to flag down the waiter.

"Hey, guys. What can I get ya?"

As we rattle off orders, me copying McKenna's and reaffirming Reece's earlier claim, my mind spins around how true of a statement it is. I'd wanted to keep reaching for that stronger version of myself and tell the two most important people in my life about my decision to chase my bookstore dream. And yet, the inner pep talks I'd given myself all night about standing on my own, reaching my goals independently, opening the bookstore—they all mean nothing. A part of me is aware that the others are attempting to make amiable conversation, but I've zoned out, my mind spiraling as all the negatives creep back in.

When my thoughts finally settle, I look up at them and say, "Reece is right."

Whatever conversation they were having halts as both sets of eyes dart to me.

"About?" Reece nudges.

I look everywhere but at them, feeling itchy under their scrutiny. "McKenna takes care of me, and I take advantage of it. It makes my life easier," I mutter with a shrug.

McKenna turns her body so that she's fully facing me. "You know how to take care of yourself, friend. And you do more than enough for me. For everyone, really. You're always helping others take care of themselves."

As she finishes, I'm already shaking my head in denial. "Our friendship is one-sided and you know it. Same with you," I say to my brother. "I am a terrible friend. I am a terrible sister. There's a reason my relationships don't work out."

"Hey," Reece interrupts. "This will not turn into a self-deprecating lunch. All three of us do our best. I only said what I said to get a rise out of Blue Eyes." He reaches a hand across the table and rests it on my forearm. "I didn't mean to upset you."

I nod but then hastily shake my head, my voice dropping low. "I know. But it is still true. My brain doesn't function like yours, and I hate it. I wish I could have engaging conversations like you guys, or keep track of time or stay organized. Keep you guys from worrying all the time," I say with another shrug, the way too familiar sting of tears at the back of my eyes. "God, I feel pathetic right now. I wanted to start fresh after Joey left me for Ella and try to do things on my own for once, but you guys are reminding me that maybe it's impossible."

"Whoa, what?"

"What's going on, sweets?"

Both of them start talking over each other, and I hold up a hand. "I said I'd tell you what happened between us, but honestly, I don't feel like going into too much detail when y'all are both acting ridiculous. Three weeks ago, I found Joey and his best friend in our living room together. They've been together for a few months. I don't blame either of them. I'm a fun-sucker as proven by the two of you."

"Like hell, you can't blame them," McKenna snaps.

Reece is quietly stewing, and I realize I can't sit here. If Reece loses his cool about work or life, I can deal. But that look says he's about to go off on me for not telling him sooner about the circumstances of Joey's departure, and I can't handle being the disappointment again.

Nudging McKenna, I stammer, "Please let me out." The tears and fears and truths press in on me like walls.

"Jett, let's talk—"

My eyes must hold enough desperation in them, because she slips out of the booth.

"Keep your phone on you."

I nod at my brother's terse request without looking at either of them. As quickly as I can without running, I slip out the front door and set out on the sidewalks of Havenwood.

Chapter Seven

Jett

I'm not sure how long I walk through town. The moisture in the air teases snow flurries, and my lungs finally take in a full breath. I need more layers. My toes are freezing through my sneakers, and my fingertips may never return from their current purple color. It is too cold to wander these streets, but returning to Reece's or my house in Covington seems terrible. I try to push the thoughts of coldness away and appreciate my surroundings.

Havenwood is beautiful year-round, but the winter months are my favorite. Even just this slight bit removed from the center of the small town, the open fields and rolling hills are still green with tall fescue. Most of the trees are bare, but it just adds to the beauty, in my opinion. Preparing for a new season of life.

Further down the road, I can see the outline of River Haven Ranch. Back in the day, it was a functional cattle ranch, but now the Flynn brothers just train horses out of it. The classic red barn would make a gorgeous backdrop for someone's cover design.

Along the other side of the road is house after house, though they all have a decent amount of space between them and all have large backyards. It always amazes me how this town exists between some of the most popular tourist-attracting cities but never seems to have anyone out of the ordinary.

Everyone is always overly friendly. Everyone knows everyone else's business. And yet, out here, away from the bustle of Covington, away from the prying eyes of the citizens of Havenwood, I feel more at peace than I have in weeks. I know it'll be short lived, but I enjoy it while it lasts.

As I come upon a bench along the sidewalk on my way back toward town, I take a seat, letting my head drop into my hands, knee already bouncing. My mind spins from wanting to talk to Joey because I miss him, to going back to Riley's and giving Reece and McKenna my real thoughts on what they say and do, to wanting to cry because my life has fallen apart, to kicking myself for not getting my shit together, to the sexy, dark-haired man who saved me. The same one I told not to waste his time.

Why did I tell Noah that? Oh, right. Because it will save everyone from any disastrous outcome. Still, I continue to think about our encounters, the warmth of his hands, the light in his eyes. The way it felt like he actually saw me and not just my flaws. I have to be naive to think that, right? Is it possible for Noah—a guy I met by chance—to truly see me without knowing me?

Reece doesn't like him. Though, quite honestly, I'm not sure why I care what my brother thinks. I've always taken his opinion seriously. Growing up, the worst thing in life was when I would do something that affected Reece negatively. It always ate away at me.

His opinion still matters, but why should it hold more weight than my own? Especially when he still sees me as the teenager who couldn't stay out of detention instead of the twenty-seven-year-old who has excelled in a challenging career field.

I'm a big girl. I can hold my own against snarky clients. I pay my bills—mostly—on time. I have no student loan debt, and I paid cash for my little Ford Taurus. So, why am I still desperately trying to placate my big brother with my taste in men?

It ends today. No more people pleasing. It's time to do something that benefits me and me alone.

As I return to thinking about Noah's deep, rumbly voice and calloused hands, I swear his voice fills my ears. My head tilts, ears listening to figure out if I'm hallucinating or not. A hand on my shoulder has me jumping from the bench and cursing.

"Holy crap on a cracker. What the hell was that for? Can't you see I was in the middle of daydreaming? Hasn't anyone ever told you not to interrupt a girl when she's firmly in the land of fiction?"

As my tangent comes to an end, it clicks that Noah Slater—the star of my fantasies as of late—is standing in front of me with an adorable Australian Shepherd puppy at his side. Puppy may be an exaggeration. It's probably closer to two or three years old.

"You look troubled," he says. That damnable smile is still in place, but a hint of concern taints it just a bit. "You okay, chaos?"

Just like that, the walls around my heart reenforce themselves with steel plates at the use of a nickname that has haunted me most of my life.

"Don't call me that." I want my words to express the anguish that the term brings me because of how many times it's been used to describe every negative aspect of my personality, my habits, my life.

Instead, they come out in a rushed whisper, one I'm not even sure he can hear until he tilts his head in question, his eyes studying me a little too intently. The pup steps forward and nuzzles my hand, licking my fingertips. I welcome the distraction, scratching the top of the red merle's head.

"What's her name?" I ask with only a slight wobble in my voice.

"Sadie. What about what I just said caused you to clam up so fast?"

Shaking my head, I groan. "No one wants chaos in their life. Trust me, I'd know." I can't name the look that flashes over his face, but suddenly our bodies are much closer, Noah's chest nearly brushing mine. His hand glides up, thumb and forefinger gently gripping my chin.

"Whoever said they don't want you is full of shit and doesn't know a good thing when they see it."

For the first time in weeks, my mind is quiet. Noah's chocolate-colored eyes bore into me, not giving me a chance to argue back. Not that I could form the words right now anyway. Because when he looks at me like this, it feels possible. Like maybe he means it.

Maybe someone—Noah—could accept all the crazy that comes with me.

The little voice in the dark corner of my mind whines that if my own brother and best friend can't handle it, there is no way some random mechanic can.

He must sense the hint of hesitation, because as his hand slips away, his words allay my fears.

"There's nothing negative about my nickname for you. My life is all about order. Numbers make sense. Machines work a certain way. There's nothing to question. But the second I saw you and you opened your mouth, I was hooked. You were frazzled and ticked off but still had enough fire to spit back sarcasm."

Slipping back onto the bench and letting Sadie settle between my legs with her big boxy head on my thigh, I take a breath and look back to Noah. "It's never held a positive connotation."

One of his large hands reaches out again to slip a loose tendril of hair behind my ear before cupping my cheek. I've imagined him touching me since our romance-worthy meet-cute.

My breath catches in my throat. Surely, this is a dream. Just another part of my overactive imagination fantasizing about the perfect man. His eyes search mine for a moment before a different grin graces his features. This one is softer, full of understanding.

"Something about you calls to a piece of me that I swore was dead and buried. I know you said you weren't interested, but I'd still like to know you. Even if just as friends."

I watch this man, trying to figure out if he's toying with me or not. When I can't decide and start squirming under his scrutiny, I turn away, effectively removing his hand from my skin, and I want to whimper at the loss of contact. Both times, his touch has quieted the fifty thousand open tabs in my head. Something only alcohol and the worst of medications have ever done. Except this time, the quiet isn't numbing. It's peaceful.

"Are you a superhero?" I ask, my lips quirking up. Sure, it's cheesy. But something tells me he will appreciate the childish humor.

"Why?" he asks, his eyes alight with curiosity.

"Because you saved me from a tin can death trap, and now you're calming me down by calling me chaotic. And something about that sentence is very, very wrong."

He laughs a deep guttural laugh, startling Sadie, who had dozed off between us.

"First of all, you were never in any danger in that elevator. The power just went out. Like I told you then, the generator didn't do its job. But you were safe." He nudges my shoulder with his. "Maybe I just see you, Jett Taylor. Even though you try your best to hide."

He goes to stand, triggering Sadie to do the same, and says, "The next time we run into each other—and there will be a next time—I plan to convince you that you are worth my time. See ya later, Chaos."

And with that, he and Sadie resume their walk down the sidewalk toward town.

***

I don't know how long I remain on the bench, but at some point, my phone vibrates. I answer without checking, assuming it is my brother. "No need to worry. I'm still alive."

"I'm glad to hear that, but I'll always worry about my daughter." The voice on the other end has me pulling the phone away to check the caller ID.

The emotions swell up, clogging my throat. I bite my lip hard to silence the sob that wants to escape before responding. "Daddy."

"Everything okay, sweetheart? Trouble with your brother?"

"Nothing out of the norm. I stormed out on him when he said something I didn't agree with."

"Now, Jetpack, how are we supposed to address big feelings?" he asks, using my nickname and one of the first tactics he'd taught me growing up when I couldn't handle my emotions.

My shoulders slump as his worry seeps through the phone. "I should've talked to him. And I will. Too many big feelings this month."

"I get that, sweetheart. I do. But if you keep shutting everyone out when you're hurting, who is going to be there to take care of you?"

That's the problem, I mutter to myself. To my dad I say, "Reece and McKenna won't get along, and it makes it difficult to tell them anything. I don't have anyone else."

"You have your old man. Tell me what's going on. Is this still about Joey? We have plenty of land. No one would ever find the body. And since we used Lyme on the field this year, no one would question another purchase."

I can't help but laugh at the absurdity of my daddy murdering my ex. "I don't hate him, Daddy. I'm just still hurting."

"You're always welcome to come up to Kentucky for a bit if you need to get away. No heads up needed."

"Thanks, Dad." My voice cracks, so I clear my throat before continuing. "I'm just trying to convince everyone that I'm capable of taking care of myself." Even if it isn't true.

"I'm always here for you, baby girl. But I think you should go talk to your brother and make him see your side of whatever is eating at you. He's stubborn, but you're strong."

"Thanks, Dad. Were you calling for anything specific? I kind of snapped at you, thinking you were Reece and all."

"No, Jetpack. I just wanted to check in since I hadn't talked to you in a few days."

"Love you, Daddy."

"Love you, too. Call me soon, yeah?"

"Yes, sir."

CHAPTER EIGHT

Noah

"You look like shit, man."

I laugh, bringing the beer Jace placed in front of me to my lips. "Exactly what every man wants to hear. Thanks, bud."

Jace shakes his head as he dries glasses, his massive frame taking up the majority of space behind the bar. "You know what I mean. You look like you haven't slept in a week."

He's not wrong. This time of year, my mind goes into survival mode. During the day, I keep my hands busy. At night, I slip down to the gym by the ranch and hit the bags until my brain turns off. I'll sleep for an hour or two then do it all over again. Nothing about February is ever easy. Too much loss over the years.

When I don't answer Jace, he sets the glass down and leans against the bar to catch my eye. "Two weeks out," he says. Nothing more. He just waits.

I stare at the cowboy decor behind the bar while taking another long pull from the green bottle, knowing Jace won't add anything unless I acknowledge the date that is quickly approaching. I almost brush him off, but Jace is too intuitive for his own good and would bring us full-circle to what the month of February entails.

Giving in, I nod while trying to keep emotions from clogging my throat.

"How are you holding up?"

It's a miracle the bottle doesn't shatter with the grip I have on it. My knuckles are nearly white. I take a breath, forcing my hands to relax and pasting a smirk on my face. It isn't Jace's fault that this month holds too many rounds of trauma to count.

"Might just skip February this year," I grumble, taking a swig of beer. I've worked every allowed overtime hour for the last two weeks in an attempt to ignore the mental anguish that lives rent free this time of year. I wish there was an easy solution to this, or someone to share my struggles with. Images of green eyes and messy hair flash through my mind, but I push them away as soon as they surface.

No one deserves to get dragged through this pit with me.

"Noah."

"Jace."

My best friend sighs. "Is that really what you want? To pretend nothing's bothering you?"

"Trace and Farrah are in town staying at my mother's house for the next week or two. Mom's already called and asked when I'll be making an appearance. Oakley has been blowing up my texts between flights. Apparently, I should be overjoyed for the opportunity to spend time with family."

I can't help the bite of sarcasm that slips in. Jace is one of the few who know about my dad's death and the guilt I still carry over a decade later. I'm more than a little damaged from the things I've seen, and trying to pretend like I'm not is infinitely more difficult when under my mother's roof. She has never placed the blame on me, but seeing the heartbreak in her eyes even after all these years eats away at what is left of my heart. My brother is a different story; time has not lessened his hatred of me.

"Mama Slater loves when you visit, man."

"I'd rather her just come here, ya know? Instead of Trace spoutin' off at every turn. I'm pretty sure I'll put him through a wall if he says something to make Mama or Oaks upset, even if it is deserved."

"Take someone with you who can run interference. Hell, I can get someone to run this place for the day and go with you.

Kelsey would probably jump at the chance to spend time with your sister."

Shaking my head, I rock back and balance the barstool on two legs for a second before settling back down. "I don't need a babysitter."

"Never said you did. But you need your friends." Jace waits for me to meet his eyes before continuing. "It's okay to ask for help, man." He slides a soda in front of me, a brow arched as if daring me to argue.

"What? Am I on the Drew drinking plan, now?"

"Tired of my friends making poor decisions. Figured it's time to force y'all into better habits when I have the chance." He swipes the empty bottle from the counter and tosses it before something across the room catches his attention. "Still think if you just don't talk about the other elephant in the room, it'll magically get better?"

"Damn it, Jace," I grumble, pushing away from the bar with a half-cocked plan to storm out.

Jace quickly slips around the bar and forces me back onto my stool. "Don't storm out of here pissed at the world, man. You need to talk about her. Especially if you want to make anything happen with the little number that just walked in with her brother."

"You know it wasn't like that with Maya."

"Do I? Because you haven't been with anyone since her."

"How do you know?"

He cuts his eyes at me, that eyebrow arched.

"Yeah, okay. I haven't been with anyone in three years. So, what?"

"You need to let yourself move—"

"I have moved on."

"No. You've let grief for something that wasn't your fault keep you from finding someone who could love your surly ass. And my money says she just walked in."

At Jace's second nudge, I glance up from where I'd traced a pattern in the Coke can's condensation and slowly refocus on my surroundings. As I turn to follow his gaze, I catch sight of Jett by the community bulletin board. The farmhand follows his sister and immediately spots me, his face turning to stone. Reece's dislike of me is just one more reason to avoid seeing my brother in person any time soon.

"Ah. Her."

Jace snorts but doesn't say anything else as Reece makes his way to the bar.

The tension in the room intensifies by ten. Reece hesitates for only a second, but it is enough for Jett to notice me, too. When her green eyes find me, she gives a little wave before turning back to the board. Her hand reaches up, quickly snatching an index card off. Before hope sets in—because I'm fairly certain that was my rental card she grabbed—Reece appears beside me, blocking his sister from view.

"Your kind just can't leave well enough alone, can you, man?" he says. "She's off-limits."

Any semblance of patience and desire to be civil for Jett's benefit catapults out the window. Before I can stop it, I feel myself slip into the person I am everywhere else. Outside of Havenwood. The asshole elevator mechanic.

"My kind, huh?"

Reece steps into my space, crowding me. Wrong damn time for him to bring up Trace. I shift to my feet, the bar stool skidding across the wood floors.

"Talk shit about my family. I dare you." Even if my brother is a jackass, no one else gets to hate on him.

Reece takes another step forward, and my shoulders tense. I'm itching for a fight. Throwing a punch or two would alleviate some of the pressure, both mental and physical.

"Stay away from my sister. She's too good for you," Reece says, his voice low as he glances to make sure she isn't approaching yet.

I can't stop the laugh that slips out. "No shit, Sherlock. But it seems like you've done a shit job protecting little sister from scum not worth her time. That girl is beautiful inside and out. And yet she thinks she isn't worth *my* time. Tell me, hot shot, how a girl like her could possibly believe that? *My kind* would convince her that she is *everything*."

Some of the anger seeps out of Reece's eyes, but I'm too keyed up now to stay put. Stepping around Reece, I lock eyes with Jett, certain she heard at least some of that and not caring that she did. I hold my fist out, and she bumps it, a slight grin on her face.

"Later, chaos."

Jace stops me before I can get too far. "You goin' to Drew's?"

"I'm going to lay someone out in your bar if I don't."

He nods, glancing back at Reece. I can feel the daggers shooting into my back, but I refuse to acknowledge him any more than I already have.

"Touch base later, yeah?" Jace says.

"Will do, brother."

***

The sun is already sitting low as I walk through the door of Drew's gym. The guy lives in the upstairs loft apartment, but I'm surprised to see him downstairs. Last I heard, he still wasn't cleared to do much of anything outside of his physical therapy sessions.

As I step closer, I take in the pallor of his skin and the coating of sweat. A new tension sets into my shoulders, this one fueled by panic. I quicken my steps across the gym floor to the bench near the stairs that lead up to the loft.

"Drew, man. You okay?"

His head tilts in my direction, but his eyes aren't focusing on me.

"Hey." I snap a finger in his face.

His eyes slide to mine this time.

"Pain or withdrawal?" I hate that I even have to ask.

"Both," he pants before looking away. The strain is visible in each breath he takes as he tries not to move his torso or arms.

"Back or shoulder?"

As Drew tells me it's his shoulder, I'm already shooting off a message to his brother, knowing Declan can get here faster than Jace can.

"I don't like how pale you are, bud. Can you let me help you to the floor?"

A single nod is all he gives me.

"Cradle your arm."

As he does, I crouch beside the bench, quickly pulling Drew onto my knee and lowering us both to the rubber mats.

By the time I have his head pressed between his knees and am pulling a wet rag from the gym cooler, Declan storms in, his wife Kristen quietly slipping in behind him.

"The hell were you doing down here, Drew?"

"Declan, we talked about this. Now is not the time." How Kristen manages to scold her husband without sounding like she's ripping him a new one is impressive.

Declan stalks across the gym, hands clasped tightly behind his head.

Placing the rag on Drew's neck, I tune back in to what Kristen is saying, her tone soothing as always.

"Do you want me to call Dr. Lindsay? You know she'll make a house call for you."

"No."

Declan growls from the other end of the room but doesn't comment. I know it has to be killing him to see his brother in pain. It's sickening to see a shell of my friend.

None of us expected Drew to develop a dependency on opioids, least of all the man who treats his body like a temple. Aside from a few drunken adventures, Drew thrives on water, lean protein, boxing, and riding. Whatever happened leading up to his accident changed him. I thought he'd quit the pills cold turkey a month ago, but the bits of conversation I heard between him and Jace recently suggest it wasn't as clean cut as I'd hoped.

My gut churns as I ask, "Where's the pill bottle, Drew?"

Defeat pours from his body, but he doesn't say anything. It must be the last straw for Declan, because he storms up the steps and disappears into Drew's loft.

"You can't ride out the withdrawal and the pain together, man."

I slip up the stairs to follow Declan and hear Kristen add, "Drew, honey. I do not want to haul you down to the medical center, but if we can't get your pain level down, I won't have a choice. We can try a few pressure points if you want."

As I slip through the door, Kristen's voice fades, and I can hear Declan storming through the bedroom and what sounds suspiciously like things being thrown against a wall.

Leaning my head back out, I holler down. "You gonna tell me where to look, or are you good with your brother ransacking the entire place?"

"Sock drawer," Drew rasps.

I slip into Drew's room to find Declan on the edge of the bed, head in his hands.

The groan that wants to slip out stays contained, barely. I do not have the mental capacity to comfort grown-ass men today, no matter how important they are to me. Drawing on my last bit of patience, I retrieve the two pill containers from the top drawer of Drew's dresser before leaning against the worn furniture.

"What's on your mind, Dec?"

"You know it's my fault, right?" Declan asks.

I shake my head. "You didn't make him jump on Havoc."

The poor colt hasn't been saddled since the accident, and the only guys allowed to handle him are Declan and Reece. The thing is a skittish mess.

"Not that part. The reason he got drunk that night, though? That was all on me."

"Drew's a big boy. He made his own choices. That's not on you."

Declan nods toward the door. "He's trying to do it on his own because he doesn't want my help. And he doesn't want to talk to Kristen because she's my wife." He mumbles something else that sounds suspiciously like "stupid Leila" as he stands and slips out of the room. I bite my tongue in an effort to keep from asking questions.

Leila was Drew's childhood sweetheart. When she became the poster child for bad luck and had to leave Havenwood before she turned eighteen, it'd taken over a year for Drew to move on. How could she have anything to do with something that happened last summer?

Shrugging off the thoughts, I return to the gym to find Kristen encasing Drew's shoulder in ice packs. Some of the tightness in my neck and shoulders releases as I take in the color returning to Drew's face.

"What caused the flair up?" I ask, placing the pill containers in Kristen's awaiting hand.

"Got pissed off. Punched the bag a few times."

Declan opens his mouth, I'm sure to call his brother all sorts of words—I'm ready to as well—but Kristen stops him.

"Honey, if you aren't going to be helpful, go outside please. Drew, where is your stability brace?"

"I saw it upstairs," I mumble. "I'll grab it."

As Declan storms out, I trek back up the steps to get the brace from the bathroom. Except when I find the brace, Drew's phone is on top, screen lighting up with a text message. I try to ignore it, but the name draws me in.

> Leila: Please call me back. I can't do this alone.

"Not my business," I mumble to myself as I slip back downstairs and help Drew slide into the brace.

He looks at me. "You aren't going to tell Jace about this, right?"

Shaking my head, I grin. "Of course not, man." As Drew sighs in relief, I add, "You are."

Kristen laughs while she double-checks the straps and placement. If it were anyone else going back over my work, I'd be irritated, but Kristen did time as a trauma nurse before she transitioned to psychiatry. She knows her stuff.

Drew hangs his head.

I give his good shoulder a squeeze on my way out. "If I go gray before thirty-five, I'm blaming you."

I swear, friends in this town are good for nothing but stress. But damn, do I love them. At least I no longer have the urge to knock Reece Taylor on his ass.

Chapter Nine

Jett

"I think that's the last of it," my brother says as he slips past me with an overflowing box of my favorite blankets. The house behind him is empty, save for the appliances and years of memories that I wish I could burn.

"Okay, cool."

"You wanna do another pass through any of the rooms?" Reece asks.

"Nope. Not interested in stepping a toe over that doorframe again." I fidget with my fingers, tearing up the edge of a slightly too-long nail and cursing when it pulls too close to the quick.

The last two weeks have been slammed with packing, paperwork, trying to squeeze in conversations with potential clients, and not letting the little voice in my head talk me out of moving to Havenwood. I'd finally settled my thoughts by last night, but the anxiety kicked back in as soon as McKenna bailed on me earlier, saying she would make a coffee run. Our plan is to meet at my new loft apartment above the bar that Jace owns, but I think we are all trying to avoid stepping on each other's toes. Things have been awkward all around since that day she, Reece, and I had lunch together.

I packed all my clothes and books while Reece and Jace loaded all the heavy furniture into a "clean" livestock trailer. Trust me, I nearly had a cow (no pun intended) when Reece told me this was their plan to move everything from Covington to Havenwood in one trip. One of the brothers that he works for, Drew, tagged along with the guys, but is clearly only that—a tag-along. Something about just needing to be around people but not being able to lift anything. Jace introduced us, immediately apologizing for Drew's "surly asshole-ishness."

"Drew's not as grumbly as Noah, but it's a close second," he'd said. I'd rolled my eyes, because Noah Slater is anything but the town grump that everyone thinks he is.

Drew and I don't say much to each other. He keeps to himself, and I'm too socially awkward to start the conversation. But as the guys load the last of the boxes in behind the sofa and bed, I can see physical pain etched along his features. I may not be great at reading emotions or social settings, but I'd recognize pain anywhere. Like calls to like, and all.

I step into his line of sight. "You good?" I ask.

"Sure thing," he grunts, his eyebrows pinched together. An uncomfortable vibe rolls off him in waves, and his arm is cradled tight to his side. His breathing seems off, too.

"You don't look it, ya know. I'd say you're hurtin'."

He looks at me quizzically. "You ever break a bone?"

"Nope, but I've run into enough walls and hit my head a few times."

He lets out a breath in a huff of air. "I've got multiple breaks and fractures that refuse to heal up right but quit taking the pain meds."

"Why on God's green Earth would you do that?"

"Do what? Break things?"

I narrow my eyes at him. "Okay, smartass. Why would you quit taking pain medication if you're still hurting this much?"

He looks away, staring off toward the other guys as he says, "Your brother has mentioned over the years that you've taken medications in the past that you didn't mesh with."

"Not sure why he's sharing any of that since it's none of your business, but yeah. I can't take stimulants. So what?"

He stares at me like I am clueless. I'm not naive; my brain just doesn't process like a normal-minded individual. Why can't people just be direct?

"Look, I don't grasp things when I should, so you're better off just telling me, or we'll be here all day with me trying to pick up what you're putting down."

His laugh is low, quiet, more a breath of air, but happier than the first breath he'd done that with earlier. "You don't pull punches, do you?"

"Never learned how to."

He nods, accepting the answer. "My body formed an addiction to the pills I was on before I realized it. I cut them out cold turkey, went back to them, and then quit again last week."

"Well, damn."

A smile tugs at his lips, showing a devilish dimple.

"Makes sense," I add. "Why you're so snarly and whatnot."

Drew chokes out a laugh. "You're somethin', ain't ya?"

I roll my eyes. "In all seriousness, though, Drew. I may be all over the place ninety-seven percent of the time, but if you ever need to vent, feel free to hit me up. I might not remember half of what you tell me, and I know you've got a built-in therapist in your sister-in-law, but I know from experience that sometimes it's easier to tell someone things when you don't have ties to them."

"Thanks, but I'm good, Jett. Really."

"Understood."

The other two guys close up the trailer and lock it before walking up to us. Reece studies me for a moment before speaking.

"Looks like we've got everything loaded. You sure you don't wanna take one more pass?"

Shaking my head, I walk backward toward my car, thankful not to be stuck in the truck with the guys. "If something got left, I can buy new."

Drew lets out a low whistle, and my eyes shoot to him. "Friendship offer revoked."

"Oh, come on, Jett."

I hold up my hand and slip into the driver's seat of my Taurus. Reece pops him on the back of his head.

"Dude, what the hell?" Drew exclaims while rubbing the abused spot. Not that it was a hard hit. Reece was careful not to jostle his friend too much.

"Be nice to my sister."

Tuning them out and focusing on the road, I start the drive west. Whether this move is a chaotic choice or a smart one, I still don't know.

To new beginnings. May the chaos be controlled.

***

As promised, McKenna is waiting at my new loft, two iced coffees in hand.

Thank you, Baby Jesus. The guys should be pulling up behind me any minute, and my sanity can't handle any more talk about horses and grain bills.

"Please tell me that cup has a double shot of espresso in it. Gimme, gimme." I reach for the coffee with grabby hands, but McKenna pulls both cups out of my reach as I pout.

"No, ma'am. A regular caramel coffee has more than enough caffeine for your ass."

Taking a sip as soon as she hands it over, I moan at the sweet caramel taste but still feel like grumbling about the lack of espresso.

"At least it isn't decaf, hon. I could have done you dirty there and didn't. So, say 'thank you, McKenna, for helping to fuel my unnecessary and unhealthy caffeine addiction, even though it ruins what little focus I have.'"

I roll my eyes but mutter a thanks to my best friend between sips. McKenna goes to take a sip of hers but freezes, the straw an inch away from her face.

"What in the actual hell are you doing here?" she yells over my shoulder.

My head snaps in the direction she's glaring as the distinct laugh of Noah Slater reaches my ears. My eyes dart back and forth between the two, unease and confusion creeping into my chest.

I choose to ignore the fact that my best friend and current crush-slash-hero have some sort of history and ask Noah, "What are you doing here, elevator man?"

His lips slip into a shit-eating grin. "I live here."

My head darting side-to-side, I say, "No, you don't. This is my loft."

He points to the door next to mine. "And this is mine. Howdy, neighbor."

I almost snap at him, his unexpected appearance and the news of him being my neighbor making me anxious, but the guys pull up to the curb with all my belongings in tow before my mind can take off again. When I asked Jace the other week about the card on the town bulletin board advertising the loft for rent, he had offered to set everything up for me. Sounds like he failed to fill me in on a few important facts, like the sexy mechanic living next door.

Taking a deep breath, I step back, away from the towering male, and slink toward my brother. I can tell even from here that Reece notes the look on my face. He glances behind me, and I know immediately when he spots both individuals standing at my door.

"So much for staying away from him, I guess." I shrug at him.

"Meaning?"

"Says he lives next door. Better than a stranger, I think?"

"You good with this?" he asks while still eyeing Noah, his eyes hard, jaw set.

"Are *you* okay with it?"

His eyes soften as they take me in. "I don't like some guy living right next door to you, but Jace ripped me a new one after that night we ran into him and I tried to piss Noah off. The guy isn't at the top of my list, but it's for personal reasons. As long as you are comfortable, I can deal with it."

I nudge him and smile, although I feel more than a little nervous about having all that hotness next door all the time.

CHAPTER TEN

Noah

It's a rare day when I forget how to practice patience. My mama taught me better, but some days, my give-a-damn breaks. Today was one of those days where every little thing irritated me. I'd been in a sour mood since I woke up before dawn. Working on elevators on a weekend is never at the top of my to-do list, but our deadline is closing in. Not much choice but to go in, even if I spend the rest of the weekend irritated.

That mood disappears as soon as I catch sight of two people standing in front of my door. I can't help but laugh at the unexpected situation of seeing McKenna Monroe standing outside it with the girl who has consumed my thoughts for the last few weeks. Jett glances at me for a moment before turning her head and talking to me while looking out at the town.

"What are you doing here, elevator man?"

I can't help the grin that feels permanent around her. Panic brews in her eyes at the realization that we are neighbors now. Man, what I'd do to take a look inside her mind. I want this girl, chaos and all, even if I have no business getting anywhere near Reece Taylor's sister.

As she scampers off to her brother and Jace, I turn my attention to the brunette still next to me. Her eyes track my every move with distaste clear as the blue skies overhead.

"McKenna Monroe. What's it been? Two years? Four?" If I wasn't looking closely at McKenna, I would have missed the tick of her jaw or how that little vein pops on her neck—both traits that indicate how happy she is to see me again after all this time.

"I'm going to ask you again, Slater. What the hell are you doing here? Did your brother put you up to this?"

"I live here, princess. I wasn't kidding." Probably not the best time to mention that I own this entire strip of lofts. McKenna's never been a fan of people who flaunt their money, even if it is hard earned.

Her eyes cut over to where Jett and Reece are talking by his truck.

"Does she know who you used to spend your nights with? Does Reece?" If looks could kill, I'd be the squirrel pancake in the road that I passed earlier. The look has me chuckling again. "Still hiding your past relationships from the people who matter. Got it."

She turns her back to the people below, her voice a harsh whisper. "Keep my past mistakes to yourself, Noah. None of that needs to get back to my family." She points angrily toward Jett and Reece. "And that girl and her brother *are* family. Got it?"

I hold my hands up in surrender. "Hey, no judgment here. But I'd suggest keeping our *past encounters* to yourself as well. From what I hear, the guy you've got googly eyes for isn't a big fan of Trace either." Those deep blue eyes are going to put someone under one of these days.

I glance over her shoulder to see the three amigos unloading items from the trailer on the street. "I won't say anything to her about either scenario. We can just say I fixed your studio's elevator one time. No harm done." And it's true. Her workout studio is on our company's service route.

"Is that what we're calling almost becoming in-laws? Just fixing elevators?" She chuckles before setting her iced coffee by the door and heading down the stairs to help unload as Jett makes her way back to me.

"Want some help with your things?" I ask her, hoping she'll say yes.

One shoulder shrugs up, the same oversize sweatshirt sliding off to expose smooth, tanned skin. Instead of giving in to the urge to see how soft it is under my fingertips, I lift my eyes to hers and wait for a response.

"You don't have to help me just because we ran into each other, you know."

I nod. "Yeah, but it's the neighborly thing to do."

She snorts. "Oh, is that it? I thought you wanted in my pants."

I feign a hurt expression, but my ego takes a small hit at the insinuation. "Do you always shoot guys down before they have a chance to ask you out, or am I a special case? I'm not sure if I should take offense at such a generic rejection or feel special for receiving such special treatment from such a beautiful girl."

The slight blush overtaking her cheeks is adorable, but she turns away too quickly for me to get a good look at her expression as she slips the key into the lock and turns the knob.

As she opens the door, she turns back to me. "If you want to waste your day helping us unpack, I won't stop you. But you know nothing about me except that I got stuck in one of your elevators. My statement from the other week still stands. Don't waste your time, Noah Slater."

"You don't get to decide what I consider wasted time, Jett Taylor," I say as I step around her and unlock my own door. "Once I let Sadie out, I'll be able to help."

I can hear the tippy-tappies from her crate before I step through the door.

"Hey, Sadie Bear. You have a good day? Wanna go outside for a bit?" I keep talking to the best girl as I open her kennel, and she barrels toward the back door, her little whines stringing together as if she's having an actual conversation with me. Hell, she probably is. "You wanna stay out here for a bit, girl?"

She yips in response.

"Behave yourself," I tell her as I pull the door closed. She's not quite trustworthy to have free rein over the house. Australian Shepherds are most definitely a challenge, but I refuse to own any other breed. They are the most loyal, trustworthy, and protective companions.

When I come back out the front door and close it, Jett is standing in the doorway.

"You just leave your door open all the time?"

"It's Havenwood. What, you think someone's going to come in and steal something? I'd like to see them try it 'round here."

She stares at me like she wants to deliver a witty comeback, but she tortures that lower lip instead. I almost—*almost*—reach up to smooth it from her grip, but she steps outside again before I can.

Probably for the best.

***

I don't think Jett expects it to take as long to unpack the trailer as it does, and I know for a fact her brother would prefer that I head to my loft and avoid his sister. At least Jace is a friendly face, even if he has a tendency to overshare. Like when he tells Jett that Drew dipped out when they got back to town to meet up with Kristen.

"I don't think he'd appreciate you airing his dirty laundry like that, man," Reece says.

Jace shrugs unapologetically, and after what I learned recently about Drew, I can't say I blame him.

"We all have our issues," he says. "I am tired of him hiding behind me and his brother all the damn time."

"So, what?" Jett questions. "Does everyone in this town go to Kristen for therapy?"

I try to stifle the chuckle slipping up my throat, but Jace cuts his eyes at me as he answers. "Havenwood is all about family and community. If you aren't willing to handle your problems healthily, or you aren't willing to talk about your problems to someone, those problems tend to leak through the town's gossip channels pretty quickly. Especially the ones that sit at my bar or at the bakery across the street." Meaning gossip spreads at the Riley-owned establishments.

I watch the gears turning through Jett's eyes as her body begins to sink in on itself, her eyes becoming guarded like she just upped her mental shields with a thought.

What are you hiding, chaos?

McKenna comes out of the back hallway carrying an armful of blankets. She's been noticeably absent for the last little bit while she unpacked boxes in Jett's bedroom. She sets about organizing blankets and more pillows than I've ever seen in one room but pauses a brief moment when Jett asks if Reece is back there somewhere.

"Um, yeah. He's in the bathroom, I think," McKenna replies as she gets back to organizing.

When Reece slips quietly back into the room a few minutes later, I chance a look at Jett to see if she notices her friend's blush. When it becomes obvious Jett is clueless to what just went down with her best friend and her brother, I look over at Jace, who just shakes his head in warning.

Don't ask, he mouths at me. Turning back to the girls, he says, "Y'all wanna go down to the bar and I'll get Buck to whip up something to eat?"

That nervous air wraps around Jett again as she hesitates in her task for a split second before continuing. She's good at hiding it. I'll give her that.

"What if we get him to just throw together some burgers and bring them back up here? I could definitely go for some of Buck's grilling," I suggest to the group without taking my eyes off the green-eyed beauty that wants nothing to do with me. Hell, she's barely spoken a full sentence to me since she let me into her loft. But her eyes meet mine at my suggestion, and she nods and looks at Jace and Reece.

"Y'all good with picking it up and bringing it back here? I'm not exactly feeling the whole *social with strangers* thing tonight."

The guys agree and slip out the door after a few words with the girls. Jace asks if I want to come, too, but I tell him I need to let Sadie back in from the backyard. Jett drops onto the couch and pulls a heavy looking blanket over herself while McKenna continues unpacking some of the smaller boxes the guys didn't want to mess with, since we had no clue how to organize anything how Jett would want it.

I drift over to Jett, dropping into a squat so that I'm on the same level as her. "I need to let my dog back in. You good if I come back over to eat?" She nods, like she's in some sort of trance. I glance over at McKenna, but she isn't paying us any attention.

I try again, "Jett."

"Hmm," she murmurs, her eyes finally shooting to mine. A faint blush coats her cheeks at being caught unaware. "Sorry. Can you repeat whatever you asked?"

"I asked if you were okay with me coming back over after I let my dog back inside. You nodded, but it didn't seem like anyone was home."

"Yeah, it's fine." Her eyes dart left, and she sucks that lip in again.

This time, I don't stop my impulses. I reach forward and slide my thumb over her plump lower lip, gently separating it from the grip her teeth have on it before cupping her cheek.

"If you don't want me to, just say so, sweet girl. If you'd rather I don't come back over, I won't."

A silent sigh releases from her body, drawing some of the tension in her shoulders with it.

"Thank you," she whispers. "For giving me an out. But if you want to come hang out with the guys, that's fine. I probably won't last much longer. Today's worn me out. I have so much to still do—I know I do—but right now I just want to crash. And now I'm rambling on about things that don't concern you."

The utter look of shock and embarrassment that washes over her face is adorable. She covers her face with both sweat-shirt-covered hands and peeks between them.

"I don't mean it like that, I just meant—"

"I promise, I get it, Jett. I'll be back soon, yeah?"

She nods, dropping her hands back to her lap, but the blush remains in her cheeks. I stand and slip out the door, ignoring the questioning look I can feel McKenna shooting at me.

CHAPTER ELEVEN

Jett

I t is close to ten when everyone finally leaves. Between swearing to Reece that I'm a fully functional and capable adult and convincing McKenna I don't need her to stay the night—again, I'm a big kid now—I am pooped.

Sleep sounds amazing, yet my brain is currently bouncing around roughly eight different scenarios in my head. All of them include a ruggedly handsome mechanic that happens to live next door.

Noah left before everyone else, claiming he had to get up early in the morning. Who knows, maybe he does. All I know is I didn't want him to leave, which is messed up, because I don't even know the guy. Not past the few conversations we've had.

And I should be heartbroken. I think.

Instead, I can't get his brown eyes, scruffy beard, and dirty ball cap out of my internal video player. I want this guy. Like *want*, want. That's not a feeling I'm accustomed to.

I mean, I was attracted to Joey, but never have I ever literally felt heat build just from a few looks. Then McKenna told me he'd noticed when I zoned out while asking me a question earlier, so he made sure to have my attention before asking a second time without getting irritated. I know from experience how rare it is to find a guy not fazed by that.

Granted, it was only once. But maybe he could always be like that? I don't want to get my hopes up.

Crap.

I need to get up and do something before my thoughts consume the rest of my night. Picking up my phone and touching the screen to activate it, I realize it is already after one in the morning.

Double crap. How did I lose three hours? I'll be lucky to snag five hours of sleep at this rate. Not the worst I've ever done, but I need to get back into a routine—or I guess build a new one. New town, new me.

Isn't that how this is supposed to work?

***

By the time I fell asleep, it was almost three, so the alarm that goes off at seven has me cursing and hitting snooze. Twice. It isn't until a text comes through from my mom that I shoot up in bed. What the heck does she want? We haven't spoken since the night I ended up doing shots at Riley's.

> Mother Dearest: Hi Jett. Please call me. Love, Mom.

I scroll through my contacts and tap Reece's number, nibbling on my thumbnail as I wait for him to answer.

"Yeah?" he asks in answer. His voice is gruff, and only then does it tickle my thoughts that he's likely already stacking hay or something this morning. I bypass a hello as well and jump right into my reason for calling.

"Do you know why Mom wants me to call her?"

"Jett? What are you going on about?"

"Mom. She texted me. Told me to call her. Why?"

He sighs—a pretty regular occurrence around me. "I don't know why she texted you, Jett, but she probably just wants to talk. You haven't exactly made it easy on her."

A groan slips past my lips as I fling myself back against my pillows. "She always wants to know too much."

"She loves you and wants to make sure you are doing okay, sis. Give her a call."

My thumb hits the red button on the screen seconds before the impulse to toss my phone across the room wins out. *Toss* may not accurately convey the level of force involved. Luckily, the screen lands face-up and doesn't shatter. The last thing I need is to add replacing a broken phone to the to-do list.

I swing my legs out from under the covers, resting my bare feet on the cool wood floor. My head sinks forward into my hands, elbows on my thighs as my breaths come out in shaky bursts.

Damn it.

I shouldn't have been so snappy with Reece. It was immature to hang up on him, but I know better than to call him back right now. My chest is tight at the thought of adding an extra layer of worry to his day, so I send off a text.

> Jett: Sorry. Love you…

He leaves my message on read almost immediately. I need to get up and get moving. Otherwise, the thoughts in my head will consume my morning. I quickly slip into some sweatpants and an oversize tee before walking into my kitchen, where the to-do list McKenna and I put together last night sits next to a bottle of water and my morning vitamin regiment.

To-Do List

- Go to bakery and get breakfast
- Grocery store: list in phone notes
- Therapy @ 10
- Check email—freelance baby!
- Don't forget to eat
- Seriously, Jett. EAT!

I laugh at the last one. McKenna must've added it after I'd walked off.

After the struggle of trying to decide if I am going to get fixed up today or just go as I am, I choose the latter. Sweats and messy bun (remember, not cute) it is. I triple check to ensure I have my phone, wallet, and keys in hand before locking the door and making my way down to the sidewalk to take in the sunny small town morning.

I want to try out the bakery, because Reece raves about it, but there's so many people inside that I end up hovering outside the door for longer than intended.

"The door won't bite, you know."

I jump at the unfamiliar voice behind me and realize I'm pretty much blocking the entrance to the shop. "Sorry," I mumble before stepping aside and taking in the petite woman. And I do mean petite, even to my five-foot-four frame.

"You're Jett, right? Reece's sister?"

"How did you—"

"Right, I'm Kelsey. Jace's twin." She extends her hand in greeting, the cheeriest smile lighting her face. Are people actually this happy in the morning? And functional?

"Twin?" I realize how short my responses are, but my brain is short-circuiting.

She continues to smile as if this is completely normal conversation and says, "I know. He's a giant, and I'm barely five feet tall. He stole the height, but I stole the brains. We share the looks." She grins again. "Well, come on then. Let's go get you a good ol' Havenwood welcome coffee."

This girl literally drags me through the door, her hand gripping my forearm, and I am at a complete loss at how to react.

Do I turn and bolt?

Do I let her drag me through the bakery where people are most definitely staring?

This is a small town gossip site—Jace said as much last night. I try to take a deep breath and prepare for whatever is to come.

As soon as we are past the throng of people inside the door, I start for the line, but Kelsey drags me further into the shop, all the way to the counter, where she hops behind it and starts fixing coffee like she owns the place.

"Whatcha like? Caramel? Mocha? White chocolate peppermint? We also have pumpkin. It's delicious with a small squirt of whipped cream on top. Like eating pumpkin pie."

"Um, I don't really know. I usually do decaf caramel."

"One salted caramel decaf latte coming right up." As she sets to combining syrups and creamer and coffee, she continues to talk. "So, how do you like Havenwood? You getting used to the small town feel yet? I know Covington is still *technically* a small town, but when you have that many tourists coming in and out, it can't have the same feel."

"Um, no. It's been good so far. I struggled to sleep last night, but it's a new place, so... Has anyone ever told you you're a little more energetic than most in the morning?"

She laughs. "That's just a polite way of saying 'Chill the hell out, Kels.' But I get it. My twin tells me the same thing all the time, just not in so nice of wording." She finishes putting a lid on my coffee and grabs a straw before handing both to me. "I'd love to spend some time with you once you get more settled. I'm usually here until I close up shop at two, and then most nights I either work at Riley's or hang out there with my brother. Not many women in their twenties around here. The testosterone pool is definitely overtaking us."

"Sure, I think I'd like that."

"Perfection. Here's my card. It has my cell on it. Feel free to text me whenever you want to get together and we'll set something up."

As I take it from her, I say, "I'll shoot you a message now, because I'm likely to forget as soon as this card goes in my pocket." As I create a new message with just my name and hit send, I add, "Can I also get one of whatever you suggest to eat?"

"Absolutely, doll."

"Add it to my bill, Kels," a voice says behind me. *That* voice.

I turn around to find Noah sidling up next to the counter and note that the crowd has thinned more than a little as I've stood here talking with Kelsey. Kelsey waves a hand at him.

"It's on the house, sweet cheeks. So is yours. The normal?"

He nods. "Yes ma'am."

Once Kelsey is busy facing the back counter, Noah slips a twenty into the tip jar and winks, a finger over his smiling lips to signal me not to tell the petite sight behind the counter.

"So, how was your first night here?"

"Rough, but I rarely sleep great in new locations for the first night or two."

"I get that. I don't sleep well whenever I travel for work."

"You travel? For elevators?"

He nods. "Occasionally, I'll head up to Augusta or right over the state line into South Carolina, depending on what jobs need doing."

"Huh. Did not figure an elevator guy traveled. I guess I just assumed there was enough work around here."

"There is, technically. But going out of town generates higher pay, since it is a different region. I don't do it as much now that I have Sadie, but in my early career days, I took every opportunity."

"Makes sense."

Kelsey hands Noah his drink and gives each of us a bag of goodies, a knowing look in her eyes. "You two are cute."

"Oh, it's nothing like that," I stammer, trying to explain, but Kelsey keeps that dang smile ever present.

"Mhmm."

Noah chuckles. "Nothing going on, Kels. She's my new neighbor. That's all."

Even though it's true, his words cause a pang in my chest. It shouldn't, but it does. This man is sexy and thoughtful and spent the day just helping me yesterday, even though he had nothing to gain. Hell, Reece iced him out all day, and I know I didn't do much better—for different reasons, but still.

We turn to leave the little bakery on Main Street, and he holds the door for me and says, "Walk with me?"

Instead of answering, I just follow as he turns down a side street and leads us to a small park on the backside of the building we were just in. I check my phone and realize it's already nine, so I don't have all that much time. I say as much to Noah as we sit at a picnic table near a kids' play area.

"Already trying to ditch me, eh?"

I shake my head vehemently. "No, I just have this thing over at, um, with Kristen that McKenna helped me schedule, and I'm more than a little paranoid about missing it."

"McKenna do everything for you?"

I shrug, glancing off to the playground. The conversation with McKenna and Reece a few weeks ago is still on repeat in my head.

"Hey," Noah says, gently lifting my chin with a calloused finger so that I have no choice but to meet his gaze. "Remember, judgment free."

"It's stupid."

"Nothing you say or do could ever be stupid."

I give him a look, because he clearly doesn't know me well enough to assume that I don't say or do stupid stuff all the time.

"McKenna does my scheduling and to-do lists for me, because I'm incapable of remembering, and I get overwhelmed if I have too much to get done."

He raises his hands in a gesture suggesting he's appeasing me, removing his grip on my chin. "I maintain my statement. I've already told you I like everything I've seen, chaos. Nothing about what you just said sounded stupid to me."

I roll my eyes at the nickname that I can't seem to break him from using. I sip my coffee, moaning at the perfect blend of flavors. I almost miss the heated gaze in Noah's eyes when I look up. He looks away as soon as he sees me watching him, but the faint blush coloring his cheeks gives him away. I sit back, my shoulders slumping in defeat.

"It's really not a bright idea to pursue anything with me, Noah. You say you like my brand of crazy, but you haven't seen the half of it."

"Then let me," he says, nearly interrupting me. "We're neighbors. We can hold off on the first date thing for a bit. Let's be friends. Get to know each other in a platonic way. And then I can prove to you that you are capable of giving us a try."

"Prove that *I'm* capable?"

"Yeah. Sweetheart, I already know I'm more than willing and able to go the distance with you. But I'll wait as long as you need."

"Must be a screw loose for you, too."

"Several. It's a common trait among elevator mechanics. We're also assholes."

I can't help but laugh, because this guy is anything but. "No way that's true. You're too sweet to be anything but a gentleman."

"That's because I like you, chaos. Ask any man I work with or for, and they'll have a different story to tell. Hell, you can even ask Jace. There are days he hates me." He grins.

"I think I'd have to see it to believe it."

"I do my damnedest to keep my work life and personal life separate, so hopefully you never will."

"You don't sound like you enjoy the two different sides, so why do you do it? Act differently at work."

"If you've ever been around the trades, you'd understand."

"My dad's a retired electrician."

"Power ranger." He snorts.

I roll my eyes at the jab.

"Elevators are far superior to any other trade. Pay, benefits, everything. So, it's much more cutthroat. Tough to get in. Can't take shit from anyone unless you're willing to be under someone else's boot."

"That sounds miserable."

"Maybe, but I am great at what I do and I enjoy it. I'll deal with the negative to keep doing what I love."

"Can definitely understand the passion aspect."

"So, what do you do?"

A huff leaves me along with a shake of my head. "Lost my job a few weeks back."

"That sucks, but it doesn't answer my question."

I shrug. "I was an assistant editor for a small firm. I had been with them since college."

"Was it something you enjoyed?"

"I'm good at it."

"Okay, but I asked if you enjoy it. Is *it* your passion?"

"I don't think I ever want to work for someone else again." I look at him sheepishly. "I've always wanted to open a multifaceted bookstore. Support indie authors and help get their books out there, you know? I've read so many over the years that just don't gain enough of a following to become household names. They're phenomenal, but the only reason I found them is because I search for indie reads. I'd offer my editing services on the side, independently. Hopefully, I'd be able to sell coffee and snacks as well."

I shrug, studying my coffee cup. "I don't know. I've never been great at handling my finances, so at this point I just need something that'll pay the bills. My savings will only go so far, so I don't think I'll be trying to go out on my own any time soon."

Instead of the incredulous look McKenna always gives me or the condescending glances my brother shoots my way any time I bring up my dream, Noah just...looks...at me. No judgment. No questioning whether I'm capable. No calling me crazy.

"You should do it."

"It's not that simple."

"Sure, it is."

"You sound like my dad."

"He sounds like a smart guy. You know, aside from being an electrician and all."

Shaking my head, I check my phone again and realize how quickly time has passed with Noah. If I sit here any longer, I'll be late. "Shit, Noah, I have to go."

"You have time. Kristen's office is just a block over."

I nod, even though I hadn't realized how close this little park is to the town's physicians building. As I stand and look around, trying to figure out how to get where I need to go, Noah stands with me, hooking his arm with mine. Butterflies stir in my stomach, but I shove the metaphorical creatures down. Now is not the time.

"I'll walk you," Noah says.

Too thankful since I'd probably get lost otherwise, I let Noah lead me, and sure enough, the building I need is just a short walk away.

"Do you like hockey?" he asks suddenly.

It feels like a trick of some sort, but I nod anyway. "Only Steele Valley Voltage, since they're local. I haven't really followed any other team."

"I usually watch replays on Sundays since I don't have the option to stay up late enough during the week. Or a live game depending on the schedule. Can I interest you in joining me this week? I'll provide food and blankets?" He pulls me to a stop outside the doors to Dr. Kristen's building.

"How'd you know I like blankets?" Anything soft, fuzzy, or cuddly is what this girl dreams of.

"You had about four boxes full when we unloaded yesterday."

"Ah, that."

"So, you'll come?"

Silently wishing that is purposely a sexual innuendo but knowing it isn't, I nod. Before I can turn away to step through the doors, he drops a kiss on my forehead.

"Later, chaos."

Before I can process what just happened, he's disappeared around the corner. I sigh and slip through the door, heading to Dr. Kristen's receptionist.

CHAPTER TWELVE

Jett

"**W**hat do I wear to watch hockey?" I ask McKenna as she lounges on my bed.

I've entered panic mode and have emptied every hanger in my closet trying to find the perfect outfit for hanging out at Noah's today.

"Are you serious, Jett?"

Without looking up, I nod. "Duh. I wouldn't ask if I knew."

"Just dress for comfort. You're literally walking next door."

"But I'll look homeless." Looking up at her, I pout. "I can't pull off the bum look like you."

McKenna groans as she sits up. "Bull crap, Jenette. You are gorge. Just breathe, friend. Noah already knows you're a creature of comfort. He also doesn't care what you do or don't wear."

"How do you know?" I know I sound pathetic, but my insecurities are in full swing today. It makes no sense to me, but something about Noah quiets me. And he seems to like me, which is even crazier to me. I want to keep as much of my spiciness away from him as I can, at least for now.

"He texted me to ask what comfort foods you'd want. So, I filled him in. He was worried about making sure you were relaxed enough to have a good time. He's a good guy, Jett. An even better friend."

That has my whole body freezing, my breath catching in my lungs. "Wait, how do you know that? About being a friend? And how does he have your number?"

"Don't worry about it."

"Kens, you know that doesn't work for me." It feels like little ants crawling through my veins as my anxiety spikes, all the possible scenarios of how the two know each other building doubt. Did they date at some point? Hook up? Does she have a thing for him?

McKenna sighs, and I can already tell I won't like the next thing out of her mouth. "Look, babe. I need you to hear me when I say this, okay?"

I can't force my eyes to meet hers as my heart tries to climb up my throat, but I at least turn in her general direction.

"I met Noah several years back. Not long before you and I met, actually. I'm going to save you the details, because that story is a downer, but he helped me get out of a toxic relationship. Literally loaded me up and drove me away from the drunk asshat I was ready to marry."

So many questions swarm my thoughts as I wonder why I never knew my bestie had been engaged. She knows me well enough to recognize the curiosity she just awakened and places a hand over mine, squeezing gently. "It's a story for another time, Jett. Besides, Noah only has eyes for you."

I snort-laugh. So ladylike. "You're delusional. You know that right? And it doesn't matter where Noah's eyes are, because I already warned him off." I do my best to ignore the giant bomb my best friend just dropped on me. If I go ahead and lock it up tight, I can hopefully keep my focus on my night in.

"Put on one of your book sweatshirts. Those soft, thick leggings you are so fond of and some fuzzy socks are perfect for curling up on the couch with the man," McKenna says, a satisfied smirk lining her lips a blood rushes to my neck and cheeks.

Pushing down the urge to crawl under the covers and cancel plans, I take a deep breath. "You're sure that's not too under-dressed? It won't be weird if I show up in that?"

"Honey, you could show up in a burlap sack and he'd still have hearts for eyes." She stands, putting her hands on my shoulders and squeezing. "You got this, girl."

***

I take a deep breath and knock before I chicken out. Sadie's pitter-patter and a soft whine on the other side of the door greet me.

Honestly, the fact that he has a puppy for me to snuggle makes my anxiety drop just a touch—like, a minuscule amount, but that's better than nothing, right? When the door opens, my brain short-circuits and I am momentarily distracted by the sight before me. Oh, who am I kidding? I'm always distracted. But seriously. Dark curls are free of a hat and look like fingers have haphazardly teased them. The gray V-neck and well-worn Wranglers hug his body in all the right places.

Oh, man. Bare feet. Didn't know that was a turn-on for me until right this minute.

I let myself ogle for a second longer, both confirming internally that McKenna was right about comfort and embarrassed to look up, because I can feel those chocolate eyes reading me like a book.

"You made it."

I jump as Noah speaks at the same time Sadie rushes forward to nudge my hand, demanding pets.

He steps back, ushering me inside. "Get out of the cold. Come make yourself at home. I was just putting some snacks in bowls."

As he steps back into the kitchen, I take in Noah's loft. It has an open kitchen and living room. I'd bet money that the hallway leads to the bathroom and bedroom just like mine. His space is just much, much more organized.

"Feel free to go ahead and get settled in the living room. Or you can come in here with me. Either way."

"Cool, cool." I hang out awkwardly between the two areas, fidgeting with the sleeve of my sweatshirt.

"Jett."

"Hmm?"

He steps in front of me, not touching but sort of squatting down until we are eye to eye. "What would make you more comfortable right now?"

"Oh, I'm not uncomfortable. I swear." Lies. I'm so freaking nervous right now.

"Don't lie, chaos. Your whole body is tense, and your eyes keep shooting over to the door like you're ready to bolt."

Fireballs. He shouldn't be able to read me this easily. He doesn't know me!

I want this to work. I want to get to know Noah. I want...him. My heart is pounding, and he's right. I have been thinking about bolting already. But this time, I let my impulses win.

"This'll sound crazy, but can you, um, maybe just like, put your hand on me? For some reason your touch relaxed me the other day, and I need something to ground me before I go hide somewhere and embarrass myself."

I can't place the emotion that flickers through his eyes, but the gentle lift of his lips has my insides squirming.

"You mean like this?" He steps closer and slips his calloused fingers over my bicep, over my shoulder, and rests it along the collar of my sweatshirt. The slightest increase in pressure has my eyes fluttering. Damn, this man.

"How do you do that? Calm everything?"

"All I'm doing is giving your brain something else to focus on."

"Never stop." My eyes pop open. "Shit, I said that out loud, didn't I?"

"Yeah, chaos." He gently squeezes one more time before letting his hand slide back down to grip my fingers in his. "And for the record, I don't want to stop. The ball is in your court." He steps back around the counter and dumps a small cookie sheet of pigs-in-a-blanket into a large bowl. Then he carries it and another container toward the couch. "It's not much, but McKenna said these were some of your favorites. Figured they'd be easy snacks."

He motions to the piggies and the batch of chocolate chip cookies before queuing up the game recording and pressing play. The puck drops on the screen, and Voltage wins the face-off. "Gonna grab some drinks really quick. Water, soda, or electrolytes?" Noah asks as I sink deep into the couch cushions.

"Any chance soda includes Dr. Pepper?"

"But of course." He grins and steps out of sight. "Best soda out there." As he comes back around with two soda cans in hand, he asks, "Pepsi or Coke if this is not an option?"

"Either." I shrug. "Depends on which one passes the flavor test for me at the time. But if I have a choice, it'll always be Dr. Pepper."

"Pepsi is too sweet for me, but to each their own."

"So, I guess you'd choose salty over sweet then?"

He sinks down on the cushion next to me and pops the tab on my can before handing to me. "Mmm, depends on the sweet thing. But if we're talking foods, I'll go with salty."

"I have a sweet tooth," I say, trying to soak up some of his body heat without being obvious.

"Favorite food? I'm talking actual meal, here. Not snacks, not processed sugars."

I cut my eyes at him. "Since you knocked my favorite food groups out of the acceptable answers, I guess chicken nachos take the cake." I glance back up to the screen that neither of us are paying much attention to just in time to see Voltage's number thirty-two score.

"I can get behind Mexican food any day. Especially if there's extra queso included."

"I tend to fixate on food. So, I could eat the same thing for three weeks and not even think about another dish. Grilled chicken, fresh tomatoes, and queso on top of some corn chips is one dish I can always count on to be satisfying. What is your favorite?"

"I'm a pasta lover, but an extra cheesy lasagna is my favorite. Has to be homemade, and it's even tastier on day two." He hands me a cookie and continues with his questions.

As we keep sharing small tidbits of our lives, I grow more and more comfortable in his space. There are no awkward silences, no forced laughs or uncomfortable questions.

"On our coffee date—"

"Not a date."

Noah is unphased by the interruption. "When you were talking about your dreams. Have you put any feelers out around town?"

I shake my head in response. "I don't see anyone here taking a chance on an outsider. But no, I haven't looked into any locations yet. I think I'm just going to focus on the freelancing thing. I'm more so just worried about bills, you know? My savings can cover me for a little while, but they aren't indefinite."

"If nothing else, both the bar and the café are always looking for help."

We sit in silence for a few minutes, Sadie at our feet. My eyes keep glancing to the corner chair where a pile of blankets sit. Without realizing it, I'm gravitating toward them, searching for one that is soft enough.

"Are you touch-testing my blankets?" Noah asks, startling me.

I freeze in my pursuit of pulling the fluffy cream and deep purple one from the bottom of the stack.

"Blankets are my weakness. I didn't realize I'd even moved. It's just habit." Embarrassed, I sit back down without the blanket.

"I didn't mean to call you out on it. Are any of them what you were wanting? I have more in the hall closet that you're welcome to."

"It's okay. I'm good." My cheeks and ears heat, and I know my face is red from getting caught in a crazy person moment.

Noah studies me for a moment before leaning forward and grabbing the blanket I had been eying while I try to disappear into the leather of the couch.

Before I can process Noah's intentions, he drapes the blanket over me, leaning close to tuck the edges under my body in a cocoon. The deep sigh of contentment that his actions pull from my body has no chance of being silenced, and the tilt of Noah's lips confirms it doesn't go unnoticed.

"Stop with the people pleasing bullshit, Jett. You want something? You tell me. No judgment, ever. Got me?"

The seriousness in Noah's gaze is intense, but I fight the urge to look away. Instead, I nod and let the weight of the blanket and the lingering smell of teakwood settle my soul.

"Now, why this blanket? There's at least five right there, and this seems to be the only one that passed your test."

Pulling the blanket up higher, I covertly breathe in the scent of Noah again before answering. "It just feels right." Sitting a little straighter, I add, "I don't know how to exp—"

Noah holds up his hand to stop me. "You don't owe me—or anyone—an explanation. If it feels right, that's all that matters."

I stare at this ruggedly handsome man who somehow fell into my life at the most inopportune time and can't help myself. "Who are you?"

He chuckles, draping his arm over the back of the couch. For once, I don't think. I just let myself react, leaning into the offered contact. I sink into his side as he answers.

"I'm just a dumb elevator guy who hates people."

"Well, if that wasn't self-deprecating, then I don't know what is."

His hand gently palms the top of my head, effectively holding me close. "Funny, funny girl."

I glance up. "That's a good musical. Hey, did you know number thirty-two is actually from Steele Valley? I met him a few times before he went to the big leagues."

CHAPTER THIRTEEN

Noah

"Yeah, I know Harrison. He's a cool guy."

The look on her face is priceless as Jett shoots up from the blanket, her jaw slack.

"Wait. You know Silas Harrison? Like, *know* him?"

Chuckling, I slip my arm off the couch and pull her closer. "We grew up together. He and my sister dated for a while."

I thought he and Oakley were solid. Hell, I expected him to put a ring on her finger pretty quickly, but they split right before he signed his entry-level contract. Oaks still won't discuss it, so I'm clueless about what went down between them. I know she still keeps up with his games, and he always asks how she's doing when we talk, but both of them remain tight-lipped about anything else.

Jett is still awestruck as I turn my focus back to the game. Or so she thinks. I can't stop watching her.

This girl.

She isn't mine—yet—but I already don't want to let her go. I have never fallen this fast for someone. I rarely enjoy the company of others, found family excluded. Even then, it usually takes months of constant interaction, getting to know them on a deeper level, and connecting with them emotionally.

But *this girl.* This chaotic windstorm in pint-size packaging owns me on a level that is terrifying for a man who has experienced as much loss as I have.

For weeks, I have been battling my instincts, certain that logic would win out. Emotional connections do not happen at first glance. Love at first sight is a sham. Something that sells in the box office.

Except, it isn't. Because I have been in love with Jett Taylor since the words "holy fireballs" slipped through her plump little lips. And as she sits here curled into my side while watching my childhood best friend lead his team to victory, I pray she will let me into her beautiful mind someday soon.

***

A crash followed by Sadie's whimpering wakes me from a dead sleep.

I lay still for a few seconds, trying to gain my bearings. It isn't until another crash is followed by the sweetest voice yelling profanity that I realize it's coming from Jett's loft. The realization kicks me into gear as I toss the covers off and rush toward the front door, grabbing my set of spares from the hook by the coat rack.

I'm not a creeper. I do knock. Twice, actually. But after a minute of Jett not opening the door, my patience runs out and I use my key.

I have never been more out of my league than I am right now. Jett and I have the same floor plan, but where mine is organized, clean, and minimalist, Jett's is living up to my nickname for her. Pure and total chaos. It looks like a bomb went off. Everything from blankets to pens and notebooks to shoes and clothes cover the entire kitchen and living room areas. A few containers are dumped onto their sides. I assume that's what caused the crashing sounds.

"Jett? Everything okay?" I ask, taking in her appearance. She is still in the same clothes as earlier, and every ounce of her screams *frazzled*.

"What the hell? You can't just break into my apartment. Can't you see I'm busy?"

I stay put, not saying anything. My face must look at least a little shocked. I can honestly say I was not expecting pure fire when I walked in.

"Ah, hell." Jett turns away from me, tugging on her messy ponytail. "This is exactly what I never wanted you to see."

Taking the opportunity to step closer, I gently grip Jett's shoulder and turn her toward me. As I cradle her cheeks in my hands, I can't help but marvel at how delicate she is compared to me.

"It's three in the morning, and it sounded like someone had broken in. What's going on?"

Her ears and cheeks have taken on a shade of pink that makes me want to never let her go as she fights back the moisture gathering in her eyes. I'd give anything to know what caused the spice to come out full force, but that can wait until whatever caused her panic is handled.

"Jett," I whisper while tucking a loose hair behind her ear.

She leans into my palm but finally answers. "Squishy is missing."

That's...not what I was expecting. "Squishy?"

"Yes, Squishy."

I don't try to stop the grin that spreads. "And what exactly is 'Squishy?'"

The blush that was fading quickly resurfaces.

"Nothing. It's fine. You can go."

Finally giving into the urge, I pull her close and wrap my arms around her. "No judgment, remember? Whatever Squishy is, I will help you look." The sweet satisfaction of her burying her head deeper into my chest as she answers is the highlight of my year so far.

"It is a round character pillow that's made of some kind of squishy material. Bright purple and turquoise. It was in a doom pile, but I don't know which one."

"Hell, I don't know what a doom pile is, but I'm fairly certain Squishy is hiding under that big pile of yarn in the corner."

Jett spins so fast, I expect her to tumble over. As her eyes locate the brightly colored item, her shoulders sag in relief. The sweetest smile when she looks back at me with thanks is worth the lack of sleep.

With the pillow squeezed against her chest, she slinks back into my arms, letting me hug her close.

"Want to talk about what caused the dumping of doom boxes at three in the morning?" I press. I don't want to push her too much, but she needs to get whatever triggered this off her chest. I won't let her stew in her thoughts if I can help it. Instead of fighting me on it, though, Jett spills.

"Joey, my ex, texted me wanting to meet up and talk. Apparently, he has things he wants to get off his chest." I think the laugh she lets loose is supposed to be sarcastic, but it just sounds sad.

"Do you want to talk to him?"

She shakes her head against my chest, and I can't help but hold her closer, kissing the top of her head.

"Do you want to hear what he has to say?"

Again, she shakes her head.

"Then don't."

"It's not that simple."

"Oh, but it is. 'No' is a full sentence. If you don't want to do something, that's all there is to it. No one can force you into it. We don't need people-pleasers. We need self-pleasers."

She keeps shaking her head, not looking at me. "He was good to me. Kept me on track. Tolerated me."

"I'm gonna have to stop you right there, sweetheart."

"What do you mean *stop me*?" She glances up through her lashes, and I want to beat the guy senseless for causing such self-doubt in such a phenomenal human being.

"Listen carefully to me. Commit these words to your memory. You are beautiful, inside and out. Anyone who isn't cherishing every ounce of you doesn't deserve to breathe the same air as you."

Our bodies are so close now from me pulling her against me that a piece of paper would not fit between us as I stare deep into those gorgeous green eyes, taking in the golden flecks.

"Embrace the chaos."

CHAPTER FOURTEEN

Jett

*E*mbrace the chaos.

Taking comfort from the hand on my hip and confidence from the fact that Noah didn't bolt at his first glimpse of my meltdown. I do it. I embrace it.

I rise up on tiptoes while simultaneously tangling a hand in the hair at the nape of his neck. It's a gentle brushing of lips, barely classifying as a kiss, but it sets off dynamite inside my chest.

I've never felt anything like it.

I settle back onto my heels, taking in the heat of Noah's gaze. He has not made his desires to build something with me a secret. I'm not that naive. Whether it is a relationship or just getting in my pants, I know he's doing the friend thing with alternative motives. Maybe that's why I am comfortable being this bold, because it is definitely out of character for my typical self.

"You're playing a dangerous game, chaos." Those calloused fingers skim the exposed skin along my shoulder.

"Who says I'm playing?" I ask, leaning up again to kiss the scruff along his jaw.

Strong hands travel down my sides and grip my waist before his lips find mine again, his tongue gliding along my bottom lip.

"Temptress."

Is it hot in here? It has to be. That's why it feels like someone just set my insides on fire. Joey never made me feel like this. I wonder if he feels like this when he kisses Ella?

Damn it. What is wrong with me?

"Where'd you go, Jett?"

I shake my head, not wanting to answer. Not wanting to tell him that my mind drifted. My eyes close to block out the shame and embarrassment. Just another reason Joey didn't want to be intimate with me.

One giant hand slides up my spine to grip my ponytail and tug it firmly. My eyes snap open, jaw dropping and ready to rip him a new one. Except that ass-chewing comes out as a whimper instead.

"You in your own head, pretty girl?"

Cue the weak knees.

Nodding, I sink into Noah's hold, letting his presence steady me. The bulge now pressing into my stomach proves I'm not the only one affected by this situation. Holy fireballs—that thing is impressive. My fingers drift lower on their own accord, lightly tracing the band of his jeans. Noah isn't muscled to the extreme, but I can just make out the V of his lower abs with my knuckles. It is comforting being intimate with someone who isn't sculpted.

I don't hate my body. I have a decent athletic frame and my ass fills my jeans nicely, but it is so much more enjoyable to snuggle up to someone when they aren't hard as stone.

Damn it, I'm doing it again. Just like Joey said—never present. I groan, my forehead falling to rest on Noah's chest.

"Eyes on me, chaos." His hand loosened its hold at some point, and he lifts the other hand to work my hair tie from the mess of tangles before massaging my scalp and letting my unkempt hair fall around my shoulders. As crazy as it seems, this feels more intimate than the kisses we just shared. When I finally force my gaze up to his again at his request, my insides melt at the adoration in his gaze. Why couldn't I have found Noah years ago?

"There she is. My chaos."

"Yours?" I ask, silently hoping he means it. Hoping tonight isn't a one-off but knowing I'll wake up in a few hours embarrassed and hiding from this angel of a man. Kicking back every negative thought, I add, "Prove it."

Noah shakes his head, and I can't help but lose the ounce of confidence that has been driving this bus.

"If you wake up in the morning and still feel the same once your thoughts have settled, then yes." His hand cups my cheek, running a thumb along it. "I won't be a distraction for you. When I finally get to sink into you, it'll be because you can't think of anything but stretching that tight little body around me."

Shivering at the thought, I glare at him, the look at odds with the way his words play my body. "You can't say things like that when you aren't planning to follow through on them."

"You like when I talk dirty, pretty girl?"

Heat fills my face, but I force myself to keep eye contact as I answer honestly. "Apparently. This is new for me."

He hums appreciatively. "I'll keep that in mind. Now, how about you go lie down and I'll lock up on my way out?"

"Stay. Please."

He nods. "I can do that. I just need to go put Sadie in her crate."

"Why not bring her back with you?"

"You sure? She's a bed hog."

"Hmm. I'm sure," I mumble sleepily.

Noah kisses my forehead before turning me around, gently smacking my butt.

"Go. I'll be back in a few."

In no time, I hear the pitter-patter of Sadie's nails on the wood flooring. Then there's a giant fluff ball on the bed licking my face.

Giggling, I scratch under her leather collar. "Hey, sweet girl. Are you ready for our slumber party?"

She yips before spinning around and plopping down on the quilt at the foot of the bed like she knows exactly what I just said. The light in the hallway cuts off, and then Noah is standing in my doorway.

"When I was over earlier, you asked if I'd put out any feelers for a place to set up shop."

Nodding, he leans against the frame instead of coming closer to my bed. "Glad to see you thinking about it."

"Aside from my dad, everyone has always joked that it's just a pipe dream. But now that I have the option to actually make that dream a reality?" I shrug, studying Sadie's coat a little too closely to avoid Noah's knowing gaze. "You can definitely say no, but I was hoping you might be willing to help me find somewhere." Looking up, I brace myself for the laughter that always follows these types of discussions but am met with silence. That may be worse. The urge to keep talking, to explain my thoughts or backtrack, is strong. Before I can, though, Noah eases my worries.

"I may have a few ideas in mind. I'll put some feelers out and let you know what I find." My eyes must be as wide as saucers, because Noah finally walks toward the bed and sits on the edge. "I see those wheels turning, and it kills a part of me that my support surprises you. I'd suggest talking to Kelsey Riley about it, too, if you're looking for a business partner. She's talked about adding to the café on more than a few occasions over the years."

"You just spewed all that like it's such a simple task."

"Not a simple one, but I think you have the capability to make that dream a reality. If it's costs you are worried about, I'd be glad to crunch numbers with you, too."

"Ah, you're a math geek."

"Guilty."

"You really think I can do it?"

"Whoever told you that it was just a pipe dream underestimated your heart. I can see the love for that store in your eyes even though it's just a dream. Imagine proving all the naysayers wrong by making it a reality."

Butterflies flit around my stomach at the thought of someone believing in me. My dad doesn't count—he's always supported my crazy dreams—but having someone else, someone

I genuinely care about, believing in me? No one else ever has. I start to tell Noah as much.

"Reece doesn't think—"

"Quite honestly, chaos, I don't have much nice to say about your brother right now. So, if you tell me that he doesn't support you, I may not reply kindly."

The fluttering in my stomach turns into a full-on swarm of wings that warms me from the inside out. Noah's eyes never leave mine.

He finally settles against the headboard but stays on top of my fluffy purple comforter. "Now, come snuggle and get some shuteye."

I huff out an aggravated breath, although I don't mean it. "You could at least get under the covers with me." As I lean into him, he wraps an arm around me, securing me to his side. I toss a leg across his thighs and trace circles over his sleep shirt.

"You grossly overestimate my self-control. It's taking everything I have not to strip us both and have my way with you."

Groaning, I hide my face as best I can. "Not helping things, Noah."

His laugh is infectious, making me giggle along with him.

"Okay, okay. No more. I promise." He squeezes me and kisses my head again. "Sweet dreams, chaos."

Sadie yips once from the foot of the bed as if to say good night as well.

A girl could get used to this. That's what makes a man like Noah Slater so dangerous.

CHAPTER FIFTEEN

Noah

Usually, there's nothing better than lounging on the couch with Sadie curled on my feet on my day off. This weekend is different. It's the anniversary of when everything changed sixteen years ago. Where I would normally make plans to hang out with the guys—or more recently, Jett—I plan to spend this Friday right here, hiding from the world.

I've actively avoided Jace for the last few days, ignored my sister's calls and texts, and only gone around town for the necessities. That's why it doesn't surprise me to see Drew's name flash across my phone screen. My head falls back onto the couch cushion as I groan; he no doubt needs farm help, and I'd bet anything Jace set it up. It's supposed to be my day off. I worked four twelve-hour days this week and just want to stew in my misery.

Wiping my hands over my face, I answer. "Hello?"

"Hey, man," Drew says, the sound of the tractor audible through the speaker. "We had a load of hay come in today that wasn't supposed to arrive until next week, and the rain is coming in by lunch. Any chance you'd be willing to come sling some bales for me?"

"How many bales are we talkin', Drew?" I dread the answer, already rubbing my knee. There's a reason I don't help on the ranch as much as I did in my teens and early twenties—it's called arthritis, and my knee is full of it. But hey. It only hurts until the pain stops, right?

"Looks like at least eight bundles, so a little under one seventy."

"You got other help?" I ask, like I'm not already slipping on my boots and hooking Sadie's leash to her collar. Even still, if it's just me, one hundred seventy bales is a lot of lifting and slinging.

"Heh, yeah. There're a few guys over here, but only one has a clue what he's doing. Appreciate you coming, man. See you soon." The bastard hangs up before I can add anything else.

***

What Drew failed to mention on the phone is that the only guy helping him unload hay is Reece Taylor. I shouldn't be surprised, seeing as he is Declan's right-hand man. As Drew walks closer to me, I cue Sadie to sit. She obeys, but her entire body wiggles with the desire to reach Drew.

"You're an ass. You do know that right?"

The bastard laughs out loud. "I knew if I admitted that he was here, I would have a harder time getting your help." He sobers, adjusting the straps on his shoulder brace. "Declan had to take care of some things out of town. I promised him that things were covered here. Of course, that all goes to shit as soon as he hits the interstate."

"You know I've got your back, man."

"Appreciate it, bud."

"Where do you want me?" I ask as I unhook Sadie's leash.

"Can you start stacking it? About eight high. We already pulled the older bales forward."

"By 'we,' I hope you mean Reece," I grumble, cutting my eyes at him.

He rolls his eyes but nods. "You'd think someone as grumpy as you would care less about my wellbeing."

My cheek twitches with what could almost be classified as a smile. "For some reason, you've found yourself on my give-a-shit list. Fifteen years and counting." I motion toward his shoulder. "Hangin' in there? I know I overstepped in calling—"

"Glad you did, man. But yeah, things are okay. Thanks for not breathing down my neck like Dec and Jace."

Nodding, I start for the hay trailer where Reece is glaring at the bales he tosses. Probably imagining they are me. I holler back at Drew over my shoulder. "You don't need babysitting. Neither do we. I promise not to off your brother's favorite worker. Go worry about things elsewhere."

Reece and I don't speak past a well-placed grunt here or there, but we do manage to work through the bales quickly, barely getting the trailer unloaded before the downpour. Our clothes soak through quickly as the first big drops come down hard, and we sprint for the shelter of the main barn. While I want to chew this guy out for how he treats Jett, I want him to be the one to break the ice. It only takes a few minutes of being trapped under the awning for him to crack.

"I wanted you to stay away from my sister."

I scoff. "Quite frankly, your opinion doesn't matter. She's a big girl who can make her own decisions."

"I know that." He kicks at the dirt, rain droplets still trickling from his cowboy hat.

"Do you? Because from what I've seen, you treat her like a child."

Reece turns, stepping into my space much like he did at the bar during our last confrontation. His bulk probably intimidates most, but it isn't as impressive as Jace's. When you've been slung to the mat by that freight train, not much can phase you size-wise.

"You think you understand the situation so well? After knowing her less than a month? I've already heard it from Jace that you're a good guy. I get that I may have let my past with your brother color how I saw you at first. For that, I apologize. But you don't know my sister well enough to run your mouth on how I treat her."

The grief that lives rent free in me is begging for an outlet, but I refuse to let it dictate the here and now. No matter how I feel about him, things with Jett are too fragile. I need to keep my head straight. For Jett. I repeat it over and over in my head until I'm sure I won't explode.

"I have a little sister. I understand the need to protect, care for, and even baby her at times. But come on, man. I've seen enough to know you act more like an overbearing father to a rambunctious teenager."

"You've spent time with her. From what I've heard, a good bit of time. Surely, you've seen how she gets when her ADHD flares up. She needs—"

"She's perfect. What she needs is her brother's support of her dreams." I push off the post I'd been leaning against, forcing Reece to take a step back. "She *needs* to stop trying to please her brother at every turn."

Looking out over the fields as the rain finally slows, I try to let go of the tension in my shoulders. Reece stays quiet, hopefully sifting through any recent interactions with his sister and seeing the truth in my words.

"This weekend marks sixteen years since my dad was killed. For the first time since that night, I don't want to go home and drink myself into oblivion. I'm finding myself again because of your sister." I wait until he makes eye contact to continue. He needs to hear me. "That girl is the brightest star on my darkest night. Every impulse, every blanket in every corner of my apartment, every three a.m. search for a random pillow or book or sweatshirt. Jett is worth all of it and more, and I'll be damned if I let you or anyone else dim her spark."

"You love her." He says it matter-of-factly, as if there's no question. It's such a contrast from how this conversation began that I'm thrown off-kilter but still nod once. "And I was wrong. You know her better in a few weeks than any other guy she's dated did in months."

"She's special."

"I know it's just words, but I'm sorry about your dad. Loss never really gets easier." He holds out his hand in offering. As I grasp his, he says, "I'll talk to Jett. She's been avoiding me for a while now. I'm guessing whatever dream you're talking about has something to do with it."

"Don't shut her down. Let her share with you and then discuss it like two adults. She deserves at least that much."

Reece tips his hat. "I may be questioning some things right now, but I doubt my sister is making things easy on you after her asshole ex. She's really good at pushing people away. Don't let her."

"She won't get rid of me that easily." I'm done hiding from my feelings.

CHAPTER SIXTEEN

Jett

Noah: So, what would you name it?

Jett: Name what?

Noah: Your bookstore.

Jett: Oh.

Jett: The Write Brew…get it?

Jett: Maybe not. Maybe it's too cheesy.

Noah: Not at all. I like it.

Jett: You think Kelsey will, too?

Noah: She'll love the play on words.

"Come on, Jett. Talk to me," Reece begs from next to me on the sidewalk.

I did my best to avoid him these last few weeks. Things have been tense between us since the we had lunch together with McKenna. I do my best not to let the truth hurt so much, but then things randomly crash back down around me. Up until he said those things, I would have called McKenna and had her rescue me, but now Reece's words keep coming back to haunt me and I just stew in my misery instead.

Once I realize my brother isn't going to let this go, I stop on a sigh and turn to look up at him, eyes identical to mine silently begging for forgiveness. "What do you want me to say, Reece?"

His shoulders droop. "You haven't been over for dinner in weeks. You keep sending my calls to voicemail. You never called Mom the other week, either. I know you are owed an enormous apology and that I haven't been the brother you need, but please don't stay mad at me."

"I'm not mad," I mutter, looking past him. When I notice my fingers fidgeting with the hem of my shirt, I fist my hands and cross my arms over my chest.

My brother and I rarely argue. Even growing up, Reece was always my rock. Especially through our teen years when my daydreaming and fidgeting were at their worst. The number of times I'd get in trouble in class for zoning out and missing whatever was going on, getting called out for not paying attention.

Reece would go with me to our parents, providing a buffer between me and our mom. And since we only have eleven months separating us in age, we shared classes. Those were a godsend. But this feeling of betrayal—deserved or not—hurts, and I don't really know how to address it.

Reece groans at my response, looking up at the sky then back to me. "Then whatever you want to call it. Irritated. Upset. Displeased."

I tilt my head at his broken tone, trying my best to get a read on him. "Did you mean to hurt my feelings that day you and McKenna and I met at Riley's, or were you just trying to get under her skin?"

"What are you talking about?" he asks, looking genuinely confused.

"When I told you what happened with Joey."

"You're gonna need to be more specific, sis."

"You accused McKenna of being my keeper."

Confusion flits across his face. "She kind of is. She has been for years."

I shake my head, my heart pounding, palms tingling with sweat as I steal myself to verbalize my insecurities. I never used to get this worked up about talking to Reece, but I guess things change. "She was my rock. She kept me from losing whatever sanity I still have."

"Was?" he asks.

I refuse to meet his eyes this time.

He steps closer, placing his hands firmly on my shoulders. "I can't help if I don't know what's going on, sis."

I take a deep breath, still not looking up, and relent. "I've only talked to her a few times since then. She's been busy, and maybe you're right. Maybe it's time for me to figure out how to deal with my own shit on my own. I'm twenty-seven. I should be able to handle rough days alone by now."

"Jett..." He hesitates, leaning down so that he can search my eyes for I don't know what. "What have you been doing instead, then?"

"Like I said. Dealing," I say with a shrug. Nothing else to say, really. "Reading. Trying to focus on a handful of minor editing projects. Texting Noah. I watch hockey with him on Sundays, now," I add on a whisper, blushing.

The hurt in Reece's eyes stabs me straight in the gut, even though a small smile tugs at his lips, likely at my mention of Noah.

"I never meant to make you feel like I was judging you, Jett. I'm really sorry."

"Somewhere up here"—I tap my forehead— "I know you didn't. I just want to remind you that words hurt, especially when you're as sensitive as me."

"So...are things with you and Slater serious?"

"Are you going to keep hating him?"

He groans, head rolling back as he stares up at the clouds. "I don't *hate* the guy."

"Could have fooled me."

It's Reece's turn to look away from me. "I know he didn't deserve to be treated like that. Jace already ripped me a new one, and I've apologized to Noah."

"Really?"

"We had a good talk after slingin' some bales in the rain. Came to an understanding."

"I'm drawn to him, Reece. Like, really." I shift the conversation back to me, feeling awkward discussing my not-relationship. "He feels like that weighted blanket you got me a few birthdays ago. Like nothing can hurt me when I'm wrapped up in him." I look away, embarrassed that I shared that much. I hadn't meant to, but the words are true. Noah Slater is my save haven.

"Does Noah know that?" he asks, drawing me back in.

I shake my head. "Too scared to say it out loud to him. It'll make everything too real. He already wants to date me, but I don't think I'm ready for that."

"I saw how you were with him on move-in day. As much as I hate to admit it, he may be good for you."

I nod. "I know he is. I wish we'd found each other sooner. One touch and my mind goes quiet. But I'm still terrified that I'm diving into this too quickly. I mean, Joey and I were together for two years before things went south. What if the same happens with Noah? And we've known each other for all of six weeks."

"What if it doesn't, though? What if he proves you right and helps you go after your dream, helps you be amazing. Do you really want to go down the 'what if' rabbit hole?"

"No," I mutter stubbornly.

"Don't hate me for saying this." His hands shoot up defensively at the look I give him. "I think it's time you talked things out with Joey."

"What? No." No way am I willingly letting him stomp on my heart again.

"I'm pissed at the guy for hurting you, don't get me wrong. But you never said your piece on it all. I think that's why everything with him is still hanging over you."

"You been talking to Kristen or something?"

"I may have talked to her on occasion."

My jaw drops to the ground. It has to. No way my brother has gone to the town shrink.

"Quit letting the flies in. She's Declan's wife and a good friend. She has had more opportunities than you'd think to pick my brain."

"I guess so."

"Think about it. Talk to McKenna about it. Or even Noah. See what he thinks. You know he wants whatever is going to help you move forward with him. From the sounds of it, that man is smitten."

A blush creeps up, staining my neck and cheeks.

"I know it's not worth much, but I am sorry that my words made things more difficult for you."

"It's made me grow and figure out how to take care of myself even when things feel too tough. The hard part has been hearing your voice on repeat saying that I'm incapable of caring for myself when that was never the issue."

"I didn't realize how your relationship worked. From the outside, it always seemed like she controlled everything. I didn't realize you wanted it that way. I said it to get a rise out of McKenna, and I'm sorry."

"Thank you," I say softly.

He pulls me in for a hug. "We okay, sis?"

I nod. "Yeah. Love you."

"Love you, too. And when you have some free time,

I want to hear about which dream of yours is coming to fruition. Noah seems to think you'll rock it."

CHAPTER SEVENTEEN

Noah

"Are you sure you don't mind me dropping in tonight? I swear I don't mind crashing on Jenny's couch." Exhaustion coats my sister's voice as it drifts through my phone. Oakley just landed in Atlanta and has seventeen hours to burn before her next flight out.

I roll my eyes at her, even though she can't see me, while slipping a tray of pizza rolls out of the oven. "You know you never need to ask, Oaks."

She sighs into the line, and I can imagine her rubbing her eyes in exhaustion.

"Be careful driving down, alright? I'll see you in an hour."

"Love you, bubs."

"Love you, Oaks." With that, I hang up, neither of us saying goodbye. I snatch a pizza roll off the tray and pop it into my mouth, immediately regretting the action. "Shit!" I exclaim before spitting it back out.

"Guess it's true what they say about elevator men, then, huh?"

I jump, nearly knocking the tray off the counter at Jett's unexpected appearance. "Tryin' to kill me, chaos?" I ask with a hand to my chest, the hand that is also cradling my too-hot pizza snack. The gentle smile on her lips is almost enough to bring me to my knees.

I haven't seen her smile around town this week. Since the pillow search a few weeks back, we'd started crashing in each other's lofts a couple nights a week. The last time I'd seen her was Monday, and I had to leave for work before she woke up. And for some reason, she became a pro at avoiding me this week.

Even as I prepared our snacks, a small voice in my head kept whispering that maybe she wouldn't show up tonight. Hell, sneaking out of her bed to go to work was one of the toughest things I've done. If I'd known she'd ghost me, I'd have stayed in that bed all day with her instead.

"Told you leaving your door open was a bad idea. You never know what riffraff might sneak in unannounced."

Chuckling at the lightness cloaking her this afternoon, I resume placing the piping-hot pepperoni goodness into a bowl and grab two sodas from the fridge.

"So, what's this about elevator men?" I ask as I watch her cheeks redden, her hands wringing together in front of her and her eyes looking away from me.

"Oh, you know."

"No, I'm not sure I do." I set everything on the counter and slip around to stand in front of her, leaning my hip on one of the bar stools.

I love when Jett gets this bashful look on her face. I have no business chasing this theoretical possibility of a relationship with a girl who's made it clear she doesn't want to label whatever this is between us. And yet, when she looks at me like that—so unabashedly open with what she's thinking—I can't help but want to wrap her in my arms and hold tight.

Making sure to keep some distance between us, I motion toward the couch. "Kind of surprised you showed up."

"Is it okay that I did? I know I kinda sorta panicked and hid from you for the last few days. Just had some major thoughts to work through, and I took on another new project for one of the clients that followed me." She motions over her shoulder at the door. "I can go back to my place, no problem. Especially since it sounds like you have company coming."

Forget keeping my distance. I move closer to Jett and slip my fingers into her hair, cradling her jaw. A shaky breath leaks from her as her eyes close. When she leans ever so slightly into my hand, it's almost too much for my sanity. A weight lifts off my shoulders as my thumb glides back and forth over her porcelain skin, some of the grief I carry lessening slightly.

"There she is," I whisper as her eyes reopen. "I want you here. Oakley is my sister and doesn't count as company. But even if she did, you'd still be welcome."

She gives a near imperceptible nod before taking a breath and stepping back from me. "How's your week been? You look tired."

My head rocks side to side. I'm not sure how to address the feelings beating down on me. Even though I've battled the same feelings for years, this handful of days never gets easier. As emotions try to slip forward, I clear my throat.

"Better now that you're here."

She tucks a loose strand of her hair behind her ear, glancing around the loft to avoid looking at me. "Gotta quit with the lines, buddy."

"You love it."

She lets out a soft laugh at that, nodding. "True." As she settles into the living area, she turns on the television and queues up the hockey game from earlier before looking over the back of the couch to me. The smirk on her face is new, like she knows exactly what I'm thinking about. "As much as I'm trying to get used to those kinds of looks from you, I feel like I need to thank you."

Confusion settles in as I try to figure out what she means. "Not that I'm aware of," I say, but it's phrased more as a question.

"You stood up to my brother for me. No one has ever done that before. So, thank you."

Rubbing the back of my neck, I can feel the color creeping into my face. I'm not used to anyone voicing their gratitude. Usually, it's just expected for me to do the thing, whatever that *thing* is. I don't like to see my loved ones taken advantage of.

"Someone needed to. Did you guys talk things out?"

She nods. "Well, sort of. I'm planning to go over there on Thursday so we can talk more about my plans to open a bookstore."

I pick up the tray of now-cooled pizza rolls and join her on the couch, reaching up to snag the blanket she favorites and tossing it over her. The soft giggle as she uncovers her head melts away another dark cloud in my mind.

As she starts the game at the anthems, I slip my arm around her shoulders and settle the blanket over the both of us.

"What's on your mind, babe?"

Startling, I glance down at her. Those emerald eyes are rimmed with worry. My fingers trail over her arm trying to put both of us at ease. "What do you mean, chaos?"

"You've been staring a hole through the TV for the last ten minutes. Seems like something's got your insides all twisted up."

Pushing away thoughts of my dad and Maya as best I can, I do a round of box breathing. "Thinking too hard about tough thoughts is all."

She sits forward, turning her torso to face me and effectively removing herself from my hold. "You know, someone I look up to has been teaching me that we can either talk things through or pretend they don't exist. Which would you like to do?"

I huff out a chuckle. "You're really gonna use my own words against me?"

She shrugs, not looking the least bit contrite. "If the shoe fits..."

Slipping my hand into hers, because the lack of touch has my chest hammering again, I stare at the screen. "February is a rough month for me, the last week especially."

The tightening of her grip on my fingers in silent support urges me to continue.

"My dad died when I was just a kid. He was hit by a car while changing his tire."

Jett sinks back into me, her arms winding around my waist.

"I was in the car," I choke out, burying my nose in her hair and breathing in the lavender and eucalyptus that is purely Jett. "I was in the car and witnessed his death, and then five days after the twelve-year anniversary of his passing, the girl I was seeing was walking home from here when she was hit by a drunk driver."

Jett stays quiet. Whether it's in silent support or simply that she's speechless, I don't know. She just holds tight to me as I get a handle on my emotions.

I've tried to justify it over the years. Why he died. Why the car didn't get so much as a dent, leaving me physically untouched. Why I let Maya convince me that I didn't need to walk her home that night.

Jett tucks her head below my chin, snuggling into a possessive hold. "Makes that first night at Riley's make so much more sense, why you didn't want me walking back to Reece's alone."

I expel a shaky breath while running my fingers over Jett's scalp. "I wasn't in love with Maya—we'd only just started dating—but I let her walk out of here without me. I was exhausted from work, and she swore she'd be fine. If I'd been with her, I might have been able to push her out of the way."

"There's nothing to justify, Noah."

Silence ensues, but it is a comforting silence. A weight is lifted, having her know the darkest parts of my past.

The game is well into the second period when Jett whispers so softly that I would have missed it if she wasn't lying on me.

"I recognize your pain, but I'm thankful it wasn't you."

"I've never discussed it with anyone," I say just as quietly.

"I'm not saying you have to, I'll support whatever you want to do, but I will say from experience that seeing a therapist has made a difference for me."

Jett sits up to reach for another bite of food, and Sadie takes that as her cue to jump onto the couch. She peppers both of us in wet kisses until Jett is a bundle of giggles and scratching Sadie's ears.

"I'm sorry for avoiding you this week, especially when you were fighting such a heavy battle on your own."

I open my mouth to dispute her apology, but she stops me with a squeeze of her hand.

"Things were moving faster than I had anticipated, and I panicked. But, Noah, I want to do this—whatever *this* is—with you. I'm in."

"Yeah?"

Before she can respond, the door opens and my little sister waltzes in. "Honey, I'm home!"

I cut my eyes back to Jett. "Continue this conversation later?"

She nods, but her eyes are on the purple-haired goober.

"Oops," Oaks whispers. "Looks like I'm interrupting something."

As she glances between the two of us, I can literally see when the pieces click. She stares open mouthed at me. "Is this her? Elevator girl?"

Jett choaks on her sip of Dr. Pepper.

Palming my face, I groan. "Would you quit with the embarrassment, sis?"

The Cheshire Cat would be jealous of the grin on my sister's face as she turns her attention back to my girl. "Hi! I'm Oakley. Noah hasn't shut up about you." Reaching her hand over the couch with unmatched enthusiasm, she shakes Jett's much more tentative hand. Dropping her bag behind the couch, she sighs. "Whew, I think that's the extent of my energy drink's powers."

Chuckling at Jett's bemused expression, I officially introduce the two. "Oaks, Jett. Jett, Oakley Kate. This is my blabbermouth little sister."

"Nice to meet you, Oakley."

"Same, girl. It's always a pleasure to meet anyone who can bring the sweet side out of this one." Her gaze shifts up to the screen, and she hollers. "Go, baby, go!"

Realizing Silas just scored his second goal of the night, Jett looks to me in confusion.

"I thought you said they broke up?" Jett whispers to me.

"Yep. Still support each other, though. Like I told you, I don't know what happened," I whisper back. "While she's distracted, though. Your pace, chaos. What you say, goes. I'm all in."

"As long as you're willing to practice patience with me."

"Always."

Oaks turns back to us. "Okay, love birds. Who wants ice cream?"

CHAPTER EIGHTEEN

Jett

After staying up way too late getting to know Oakley, I slipped into Noah's bed for the night. I've never slept as well as I do when his arms cage me against him. But when I wake up, the spot next to me is empty, even though the bedside clock says it is too early for Noah's work alarm to go off.

Slipping off the bed, I grab my slipper socks from the nightstand and trudge through the loft. I pause where the hall leads into the kitchen when I hear Oakley and Noah speaking in hushed tones.

"Mom really wants to see you, No. And Trace has promised to be on his best behavior."

Noah scoffs. "That's bullshit, and you know it."

"He's trying."

"I'm not comfortable going, Oaks. I'll go for a visit once he and his girl are gone."

It's quiet for a moment except for the coffee maker.

"Farrah didn't come with him. He filed for a divorce, and she signed immediately."

"Good riddance."

"Noah," she scolds. The emotion in her voice is palpable.

I know better than to eavesdrop, but it sounds like important sibling talk and after what I learned last night, the last thing I want to do is interrupt if Noah's actually getting stuff off his chest. Unfortunately, Sadie chooses that moment to blow my cover, her pitter-patter of nails clicking along the wood floor as she runs to give me kisses.

"Hey, Sadie girl. You have good sleeps?" I ask as I scratch her favorite spot behind her left ear before walking to Noah. His hands are against the counter, fingers clenched tight and a look of frustration marring his handsome face. I slip my arms around his waist and burrow as close as I can.

"Mornin' sunshine," Noah says softly.

"Sun's not up yet. Why are y'all?" I mumble to both siblings.

"Ugh. No fair. You're cute straight out of bed, too?" Oakley complains, but a slight tilt of her lips and the gleam in her eyes makes it clear she doesn't mean it. "Seriously, though. Nerdy but cute. It suits you."

"Um, thanks?" Noah finally turns in my arms and settles his hands on my waist. "At least, I think that was a compliment." Noah chuckles, clearly amused by his sister.

"Definitely a compliment in Oakley language." Oaks explains halfheartedly, but I tune it out as Noah looks at me.

"How'd you sleep?"

It was like sleeping on a cloud with my own angel holding me close.

"Woke up without you or the furry beast, but the sleep part was decent."

The little crinkle between his eyes as he worries over my words is much cuter than it should be on a grown man. "Sorry. Oakley was originally heading out this morning, so I was planning on sending her off and rejoining you until I had to leave for work."

Oakley's chair scrapes across the floor as she stands.

"Okay, TMI, big bro. Sorry to wreck your plans."

I can do nothing to stop the blush from turning my cheeks pink, but Noah just watches me, those chocolate eyes probing deep into the locked parts of my soul.

"We still can," he whispers soft enough that only I hear, but I shake my head slightly. No way can I go back to bed with him when his sister is right. There.

The audacity of this man.

Leaning my forehead against his chest, I groan. "I think you just like making my brain a mess."

"Don't know about that, but I definitely like making you a mess," he adds, and in that moment, I wish the floor would swallow me. He says it softly, but the choked laugh from across the room sets me into a mild panic.

"He's kidding!" I yell, unable to make eye contact with her, or Noah, for that matter.

"And on that note, I'm retreating to the guest room. If anyone wants to grab a coffee with me since my flight for today was canceled, I'll be ready in thirty."

Once the door down the hall closes, I risk a peek up at Noah. "Can't believe you just said that in front of your sister."

The growing happy side of me is preening at the obvious claiming he just staked in front of her. But the broken people pleaser in me is on pins and needles trying to avoid making anyone uncomfortable.

The shit-eating grin on his face is proof he found it comical, not that I had any doubt. "You're cute when you're being bashful."

I swat his chest playfully before sinking into his hold again. I can't help but sigh at the comfort his arms provide.

"Can't believe she wants me presentable at 5:45 in the morning."

"That's Oaks for you."

"So," I hedge, unsure if it is completely out of line but feeling like I need to say something. "I may have heard a little before I came in. Everything okay?"

He sighs, eyes slipping closed as if it will block out some of his discomfort. "She wants me to go to dinner tonight. Apparently, it was part of her plan when she came in last night—guilt me into visiting our mom while my brother is in town, too."

"And you're worried."

"Hell yeah, I'm worried. Nothing ever goes well with all of us under one roof."

One of his hands toys with the band of my sweatpants absentmindedly. I can almost feel the discomfort rolling off of him in waves.

"Do you really believe that, or are you just feeling guilty?"

"Both? I don't know." He sighs, raking fingers through his hair. "When Jace initially mentioned something about it earlier this month, because being Jace, he knew I'd avoid going anywhere near Steele Valley, he suggested tagging along because of the tension between me and Trace. Doesn't matter what Oakley thinks or what T supposedly says. The guy hates me and always says something to me—usually truthful—that ends with Mom in tears and me ready to pommel the guy."

Squeezing him to me, I run my fingers up and down his spine like he usually does to me when I'm overwhelmed. Although, it's probably as much for my own nerves as I steel myself for this next offering. "Would you want that? Company, I mean."

He freezes, and I'm not convinced he's still breathing until he finally speaks again. "You'd willingly go into the lion's den with me?"

I nod, but feel my shoulders draw up, tension already settling between them.

"Gonna need more than a nod with something like this, Jett. Verbal consent. Would you really be willing to go to my mom's house to have dinner with her and my siblings?"

I hesitate for only a second as I search his eyes for any warning that he doesn't want me to tag along, but all I see is hope. And boy, is it gorgeous. His entire face comes to life with that glimmer in his eyes.

"Would it help?"

It's his turn to shrug, but the tilt of his lips says it all. "Know how you say I settle your mind, chaos?"

I nod.

"Kissing you has that same effect on me."

"Show me."

A throat clearing has me jumping back, but Noah's grip on my waist keeps me from going far. Oakley's standing in the doorway, a knowing grin on her face.

"Aren't you supposed to leave for work like"—she looks at her watch—"ten minutes ago?"

"Worry about yourself, Oaks."

"Just sayin'. What if an elevator quits working, and you aren't there to save some damsel in distress?"

He looks at me, flabbergasted. "She just never quits.

Giggling, I step into his arms for another squeeze before backing out of his grip. "I'll go if it'll make things easier for you."

"Yeah?" Suddenly, he looks years younger, vulnerable.

"Yeah."

"Wait. Did you just get him to agree to dinner?" She looks to her brother. "You're gonna go? For real?"

"I'll be home around four. Ready to leave by four thirty. That should be okay, right? It's fifty minutes to get there."

"That'll work, big brother. The three of us will be ready," she says as she scratches Sadie's ears. Noah groans as he walks out, grumbling about being trapped in the car with a rotten sister.

"So...coffee?"

"Give me five minutes to run next door and change." This girl better love me for going into public before the sun comes up.

CHAPTER NINETEEN

Noah

The entire drive home from Atlanta, I had to suppress the urge to cancel dinner. I couldn't find any reason to expose any of us to what is sure to go down. By the time I'm showered and dressed—with nearly all the black stains washed away—Oakley is rushing us to the car. After forty-five minutes in my truck with Jett in the passenger seat looking good and Oaks and Sadie in the back seat, my nerves are shot.

This is ridiculous. There's no reason I should be nervous eating dinner at Mama's house. And yet, I am. Trying to talk both girls out of staying, I turn to Jett.

"You sure you're up for this? Probably won't be too enjoyable for any of the parties involved."

Trace's black F-150 is parked by the garage. My chest aches at the thought of what he might say in front of Jett. This was a terrible idea.

Oakley shoves my seat before she slides out and clips Sadie's leash. "Quit being a big baby, big brother."

Tuning out my sister, I take in Jett's expression. Hoping it doesn't mean she's about to bolt but willing to run with her if she's changed her mind. The beast of a house in front of us is staring me down. The thought of walking through that front door has anxiety coursing through my veins more heavily than I'd anticipated. I haven't been by since Christmas, and that was only long enough to give Mama a hug and to drop off a fresh load of firewood.

"You two can stand out here and turn into human popsicles, but me and Sadie are going in. Can't wait till I'm back on flights tomorrow. At least I might luck up and find myself somewhere warmer."

As those two slip off, Jett turns her focus to me.

"You okay?" Her small hand wraps around mine and squeezes.

Taking a deep breath to settle the nerves, I give her a squeeze back. "Not sure why I'm so nervous about it. Think it's just been a heck of a month, and I'm not—" I cut myself off. "Are you sure you're good going in there? Mama may stake a claim on you, and she's not one to let go easily."

"You don't need to worry about me. I'll do whatever you need me to do, be whoever you need me to be. For tonight." Wrapping her arms around me in a hug, she buries her cold cheeks under my chin. "You've got this, elevator man."

"Yo! Y'all comin' in or what? I'm hungry and Mom says we can't fix plates till y'all come in," yells the familiar voice of my brother. Glancing up, I find his head sticking around the front door, probably trying to keep as much cold air out as he can.

Lifting a hand from Jett's back, I wave him back in the house. "Be there in just a second, Trace."

He nods before slipping back in, the door slamming behind him.

"Ready?"

"Let's go meet the fam."

***

Dinner flows smoother than expected, with Trace staying quieter than normal. Mom of course fawns over Jett, wanting to know everything about her. It doesn't matter that we told her we are just friends; she's already convinced it is forever. I love her even more for it. Jett is a rockstar, never showing any outward discomfort. The occasional touches on the arm or back are the only signs she's in over her head. Whenever it happens, I either slide my hand up and down her spine or palm the base of her neck like she likes.

Even now, standing in the kitchen while chatting with Mama, she leans into my hand as it rests between her shoulder blades. Whenever she leans more heavily against me, I give my thumb and forefinger a few squeezes. She takes a deep breath and exhales the rising anxiety. Wash, rinse, repeat.

When Trace steps back through the door after taking out the trash, the air shifts and I tense. Jett reaches her hand around my waist and leans against me.

"Hey, man. Can we talk?" My brother's voice is unsure, like he knows the likely response is no. But Jett's comforting gaze and gentle smile is the push I need to nod.

I follow him to the living room, parking in front of the fire place and hoping the flames burn the nerves away. One of the few things I miss by living in a loft is the live fireplace. Eventually, I'll move into one of my rental properties. I already have it picked out. And the fireplace is the best attribute.

Not wanting to beat around the bush, I take a settling breath before addressing Trace. "What's up?"

"Didn't think Oakley Kate would actually get you to show up tonight. Sure as hell didn't think you'd bring a girl with you."

"Wasn't planning on coming. I sure as hell wasn't planning to bring Jett. She insisted."

"She seems cool," he says as he studies the flames that flicker over the fresh logs he must have added on his way back inside.

"Jett's great."

He finally takes a breath. "Farrah and I split.

"Oaks told me."

Trace just nods along, unphased by my shortness. Impressive, really, since he's usually the first one to lose his cool. In recent years, he would have already jumped down my throat about not having the flames built up enough or not being first to do some menial task. As he continues, I do my best to focus on the version of my little brother that is standing in front of me.

I'd love nothing more for this to be real.

"Lately, I've been doing some soul searching. Started talking to someone about Dad's death, and I am realizing that most of my anger is misplaced. I've made your life hell since we were teenagers, and I'm sorry. For that. For making you feel unwelcome in our hometown, in our childhood home.

"I know you found a home in Havenwood after I all but forced you away from us. You didn't deserve any of that."

I stare in shock, not truly grasping his words. Is he serious? Am I dreaming? Is this for real?

"I'm not...I don't know what to say."

"Jace said—"

That yanks me from my stupor. "Wait, when did you talk to Jace?" I am going to murder my best friend.

Trace at least has the decency to look a little embarrassed. "Might possibly call him every now and then to check up on you. Knew you wouldn't answer my calls or texts but needed to know my big brother was doin' okay."

"Since when do you care, Trace? Since when? You've spewed nothing but hate at me since we were kids." My heart is in overdrive, pumping fiercely to match the anger—or is that hurt?—boiling over.

"Since I started getting made fun of for not having a dad."

Freezing with my hand midway through my hair, I turn back to Trace. "What do you mean?"

"Middle school was brutal. Kids realized I didn't have a dad around, and it's all the ammunition they needed. Then high school—not having him there for any of my games, gradua-tion, moving into college." He trails off before refocusing on me. "I'd associated you with the loss of him since you were there with him. I had this unrealistic expectation that you should have saved him."

"I was a—"

"A kid. I know. I *knew*. But it's taken me twelve years, a divorce, and actually talking about it out loud to even begin to sift through that grief. It's *hard*. And you've been pulling double grief duty between dad and Maya. So, I'm sorry for being a shit brother."

I turn away again; I can't keep looking at him as my eyes threaten to leak. "Why now?"

"Told you."

"No, why are you laying all this out now? This isn't your style. It's one way we have always been the same. We don't share our feelings."

"I'm trying to build a life that Dad would've been proud of. Means I have a ton of work ahead of me."

He holds his hand out to me—a clear offering that I'd be stupid not to take, even if I'm worried it may be too good to be true.

Chapter Twenty

Noah

I glance at the clock again. Six-oh-two. Jett was supposed to be here at 4:30. I reach over to scratch behind Sadie's ear as she whines at my obvious discomfort. Something isn't right. This girl has me wrapped so tightly around her finger, and she still hasn't even agreed to an actual date.

Instead, the last two months of her being my neighbor have included Voltage hockey games on Sundays, baring my soul to her, sharing a bed fully clothed, and introducing her to my entire family. Sure, she's gotten distracted and been a half hour late, but she always sets alarms. She hasn't answered the three messages I've sent, and the call I made to her cell went straight to voicemail.

Just as I'm about to give into temptation and submit to Reece's harsh tongue by calling him, my phone lights up. My excitement is short-lived when I recognize Jace's work number lighting up the screen.

I sigh, "Yeah?"

"Hey, man. Are you busy?"

"Just waitin' on Jett to show up for hockey night."

Chatter on the other end and a muted, "You're cut off," comes through the speaker.

"About that, she's drunk," Jace says over the music playing in the background.

I straighten, not believing he's telling the truth. "Who's drunk?"

"Jett. Who else?"

I end the call without another word. I stand from the couch, scratching Sadie's head again where she rests it on the armrest, and walk over to the counter, snatching up my keys before heading out and down to the bar. "Don't eat the couch, mutt," I mumble on the way out.

As I slip through the door of Riley's, my eyes immediately start searching for green eyes, but I don't find them. Instead, I find Jace's eyes already locked on me and make my way over to him at the bar.

"What the hell, man? Where's Jett?"

"She's in the back office with Kelsey."

"That answers the second part. Who the hell kept pouring drinks?"

Jace straightens into his full height in warning. I know better than to push him on alcohol intake. Of course, he takes that shit seriously.

"No, Noah. You don't get to come into my place of business and be an asshole. I called you as a courtesy when I could have easily called Reece instead." He holds my stare for another moment before I release a breath and my clenched fists. "She'd been drinking before she came here. Kelsey was working in the back, and I just came in about twenty minutes ago. My bartender didn't realize she was already intoxicated until it was too late."

My hand scrubs over my face as I try to make sense of this all. "Assuming you're wanting me to get her home?"

He shoves a thumb over his shoulder. "Kelsey's back there with her. According to your girl, boys are icky."

"She's not my girl," I automatically correct, but Jace just snorts.

"Fine, man. Go get your not-girl off my office couch before she pukes again. Otherwise, you're cleaning it."

I'd argue, but I just want to get my, erm, Jett home. I slip behind the bar and around the corner to Jace's office. I knock twice on the door frame before slipping inside to see Kelsey wiping a wet rag along Jett's forehead. Jace's twin looks up as I come into view.

"Oh, thank heavens. If I have to deal with one more bout of vomit, I may just join her on the bathroom floor."

I gently remove the cloth from Kelsey's grasp and take her place, gingerly shoving Kelsey in the opposite direction. "You shouldn't be dealing with anyone's bodily fluids."

She rolls her eyes at me. "I've been healthy for years, No. I'm fine to help a friend. Promise."

I let out a grunt of acknowledgment, my focus now solely on getting the less-than-lucid girl up to my loft. I run my fingers through Jett's loose tendrils, an even bigger red flag than the alcohol. Unless I take it down, she rarely lets her hair out of a ponytail. "Hey, gorgeous. Wakey, wakey."

Her eyes flutter open long enough to recognize me, what can only be classified as a silly grin lighting her face before her eyes slip closed again. "Sexy elevator man. Comin' to save me again?"

"Looks like it, sweet girl. I'm going to carry you home, okay?"

She hums in response, and I take that to be her consent to move her. I lift her into my arms and turn to Kelsey, who is still hanging out. "Can you open the back door for me? I'll go out the back way to keep the gossip down, but I want to know what the hell happened out there tonight."

She starts walking toward the back door to open it like I ask. "I'll make sure Jace gives you the rundown later," she offers as I slip out the door with a once again sleeping Jett in my arms.

As I make the short walk back to my backyard and slip through the gate and up the stairs to the back door, she only stirs once, sinking closer into my chest and fisting my shirt in her hand.

This girl is going to be the end for me. No doubt in my mind.

***

I'd do anything for this girl.

I have no right to that thought. Hell, I can't even convince her to label us. I know better than to pester her about it—no means no—but her reasoning for saying no isn't me. She's still convinced she isn't worth it. Whatever happened in her last relationship has her so torn up that nothing I've said has made purchase in her mind yet, but I can feel her getting more and more comfortable with me and around my place.

But the sight before me burns in a way I haven't felt before. It has me wanting answers as to why this girl was three sheets to the wind at six p.m. on a Sunday. I have Jett tucked into my bed with a towel covering the pillow and a trash can next to the bed. Sadie has curled her entire fifty-pound body behind Jett's knees, snout resting on her calves.

I already texted my boss letting him know that I would not be in tomorrow and that if he needed something, he could kiss my ass. I rarely take time off and never take sick days, so he can figure out how to survive one day without me on the job. The next text I send is to a number I never thought I'd use again. Honestly, I'm surprised it's still in my phone.

> Noah: Does Jett normally get drunk?

McKenna: Shit. Not normal but not the first time.

McKenna: Need me to drive down?

> Noah: We're good. Did not tell big brother.

McKenna: Good. Don't. I'll drive down in the morning.

I set my phone aside, pulling my gaming chair closer to the desk in my room and turning to where I can keep an eye on Jett but can see my screen as well. Silas sent an invite earlier to play our farm simulator game. When I log in, he is still playing, so I reach for my headset and make sure the volume is turned off the desktop speakers.

"Hey, hey, man. Where've you been all night?" Silas asks. Two thirty-year-olds cooped up in a bedroom playing videogames might not sound like much, but between his intense hockey schedule and my work schedule, we rarely get to connect.

I glance back over at my queen-size bed where the girl who has consumed my thoughts for months is passed out drunk. "The girl I'm tryin' to convince to give me a shot needed my help tonight. No brainer."

"Ah, gotcha. Gotcha. Is she all good?"

"Dunno. Hope so." Virtual me hops into my favorite tractor—John Deer—and starts plowing the hay field in perfectly symmetrical rows. "How the hell ya' been, H? How're things?" I ask.

"Oh, you know. Just trying to balance hockey and raising a little sister since the step-monster dropped her off last week."

My hands freeze on the controller, my tractor casually veering left. "No shit."

"Yep."

"Like, for good left? Isn't Aubrey like ten? How's she takin' it?"

"Angry at the world. And nine, but yeah. She actually told her mom to sign over all rights, because she wants nothing to do with the woman who birthed her. She'd rather travel with the hockey team than go back home. So that's been fun."

"Sounds like hell over there. If y'all want to come down just let me know. I can get one of the rentals set up for you if you want."

"Appreciate it, but I think we will keep lying low until all the court stuff blows over. Trying to expedite as much of it as we can before playoffs."

"Understood. Just know there's a whole town here that'll gladly help if you need it."

"Thanks, man." He pauses for a second, and although his character is swapping tractors on the screen, I know he's trying to piece together words he doesn't want to say. I feel it in my bones that it's about Oakley.

"I won't tell Oaks, man. Not unless you want her running to the rescue."

His sigh of relief confirms what he was trying to ask. "I don't want to interrupt her life, ya know? She'd drop everything, and I just can't."

"You don't need to explain, H. But know we are here if you need us."

We get back to focusing on the game, harvesting our crops and talking shit about each other's equipment choices until his step-sister butts in with dessert requests.

"Hey, man. I'll catch you later. The little monster needs sugar."

"Don't be a stranger."

We both log off, and I return to looking after the two princesses in my bed.

CHAPTER TWENTY-ONE

Jett

The first thing I notice when I wake up is the utter misery that is pounding away in my skull. The second is a wet tongue kissing along my forehead.

The hell did I get into last night?

As I fight to get my eyelids to open, I try to remember what happened. Once my eyes finally open and focus, my entire body freezes. Because the wet kisses belong to a dog. Noah's dog, Sadie.

"Crapola," I mutter with feeling as I try to sink even further into the coziest mattress I have ever slept in.

As soon as my eyes close again, Sadie nuzzles my neck, seeking attention. I am lazily rubbing under her collar when the air in the room shifts ever so slightly. The realization that I'm at

Noah's place instead of my own breaks through the drunk fog in my brain just as the roiling in my stomach has me pushing Sadie away as gently as I can and rushing past Noah to get into the bathroom before emptying the contents of last night's binge. As I sink closer to the floor and use the ceramic toilet seat as a pillow, the scenes from last night play on repeat.

Joey's name popping up with a text message on my phone screen.

Realizing it's been three months since everything fell apart and that I am no closer to putting myself back together.

Wishing McKenna didn't have to work the weekend so she could help talk me out of bad decisions.

Finishing off two bottles of Stella Rosa.

Calling Joey.

Calling Ella.

This time as I dry heave over someone else's toilet, a cool washcloth is placed on the back of my neck while large, warm hands rub soothing circles on my lower back. I sit back on my heels, my face burning with embarrassment at this entire situation. Before I can say anything, Noah pulls me into his arms, my back to his chest.

"Noah," I whine.

He latches his arms tighter and leans his forehead against the crown of mine. "Do you have any idea how worried I was last night when you didn't show up?"

"I'm sorry," I reply in the same soft tone he is using.

"I was getting ready to dial your brother when Jace called me."

"So, so sorry," I repeat as I give in to the desire to melt into the warmth that is Noah's body.

One of his hands gently traces some sort of circle design along my arm, and I get lost in the sensation of his touch.

"Then, when I went to rip Jace a new one for not cutting you off sooner, he informed me that you'd been more than tipsy before you even made it to the bar." The hand on my arm travels up, up, up to move my hair away from my shoulder before Noah presses a kiss on the exposed skin between my neck and shoulder. "Taking care of you and keeping you safe is difficult when I don't know what's going on in that beautiful head of yours."

I don't know what to say to him, because he is right. I keep saying I'm in this and then running at the first sign of "date" talk. All the Sunday snuggles, sleepovers, texts, and calls just add to the proof. I am tired of running from Noah Slater, and that is the most terrifying discovery I made during my drinking escapade.

"I'm scared," I whisper into the quiet bathroom while steeling myself for his response. I can feel his nod where he rests his head on my shoulder.

"I get that," he says. "I do, but I am, too."

Something resembling a snort slips out.

He spreads his legs a little, allowing me to settle more firmly into his lap, humor in his voice as he continues. "I'm serious, Jett. You know Maya's death messed me up. But you had me the second I laid eyes on you. And all these moments we've had together over the last few months have me only wanting you more. Give us a chance to thrive before ending us, chaos."

Goosebumps sprint to the surface of my arms and legs at the nickname that, coming from anyone else, would feel hurtful. But the way he says it, so gentle and commanding. *Endearing*. Like he loves that I am that way. I love it. And I love—

Nope. No. *NO.*

I do not.

I cannot.

I am not falling in love with Noah Slater. We are not to that point yet.

Taking in a deep breath while still trying not to upset my stomach and swearing I am still a wee bit drunk, I tilt my chin to try to catch Noah's eyes.

He helps by shifting ever so slightly.

"One date," I concede. Excitement dances in his dark-brown eyes, but before he can comment, I continue. "But there will be stipulations."

He tries to keep a somber expression, but the man is exuding so much happiness right now that I can't help but huff out a laugh.

"Who knew cuddling a girl who can't hold her liquor would make you this happy?"

His hand comes up to cup my cheek, thumb slowly running along my jaw. "Sweet girl, I will hold you anytime you need it. Joy, sadness, sickness, drunkenness, or just needing a hug. Don't even need to ask. My arms are always open for you."

***

A short while after our heart-to-heart on Noah's bathroom floor, he moves me to the living room wrapped in blankets. I felt my mood closing in on me and opted to stay here, although I don't think Noah would have given me the option to go home just yet. Instead, he turned on the replay of the Voltage game that we were supposed to watch last night.

"So, you really called out of work just to stay home with me all day?" I ask, not really believing him when he admits to why he stayed home today.

"I was worried about you. So is McKenna, by the way."

"You called her?"

"Text. Last night."

I groan and sink deeper into the mountain of blankets.

"Was I not supposed to? I mean, I didn't know if it was a regular habit that I just didn't know about or if something bad had happened that you were trying to drown out or what. She seemed like the best bet without roping in your brother. He's civil now, but I figured neither of us wanted him hovering."

He reaches under the bottom of the blankets and gently pulls my legs into his lap, massaging my calves with firm, sure strokes. I bite back a moan as he hits a knot and have to force myself from slipping into a daydream of him massaging other parts of me.

Like my shoulders. Those always have the worst knots. Especially the right one.

I feel a squeeze harder than the ones before it and peep over the blankets at Noah, who is staring intently at me. Heat creeps up my neck as I realize my mind slipped away from the conversation.

"I, um, didn't hear what you said," I say, the words stumbling out.

Noah continues his thorough massage and says, "I just asked if you wanted to get a shower before McKenna gets here. If so, you have about forty-five minutes."

"Honestly, taking a shower seems like a lot of work."

He looks at me quizzically. "How so?"

"What steps go into taking a shower for you?"

"Get in. Wash hair and body. Get out."

I nod along with his answers, even though just listening to them make me tired. "You have a neurotypical brain. You do things the 'normal' way," I say while using my fingers to make air quotes. "I have to get the water temperature hot enough, but not too hot, undress in what is probably a cold room with a colder floor, get in the water, wet my hair, which is super thick and long, put in and rinse out shampoo, put in conditioner and leave it for at least a few minutes, wash my body, wash my face, shave, depending on when I did last, rinse my hair while running a brush through it, because otherwise I won't brush it at all, and then turn the water off.

"Then I have to convince myself to get out of the hot shower and step back onto the cold floor to dry off and get dressed. But I can't just get dressed. I have to make sure that every part of me is dry first, because socks or pants on slightly damp skin will drive me up the wall in discomfort. And then my hair has to be brushed again and either braided or dried..." I trail off, realizing how much like a tangent this must sound to him, but I am already exhausted just thinking about it.

Noah lifts my legs and slides closer, pulling blankets away until he has me wrapped in his strong arms. "How about this," he starts, his voice rumbling along the shell of my ear. "What if you let me get the water running, and I will lay towels down on the floor and plug in a space heater in there? Then, when you're done, I'll brush and dry your hair for you."

I stare in awe at the man next to me. "How does someone like you have feelings for someone like me?"

Ignoring my question, he asks, "Would that make a shower more manageable?"

I nod, unable to speak through the emotion clogging my throat. This man. What I would do to be worthy of him.

CHAPTER TWENTY-TWO

Noah

After leaving a kiss on Jett's temple, I do as promised.

Getting the water running and laying out towels is nothing. Neither is making sure my sister's shampoo, conditioner, and body wash are all set out for her, although I wouldn't mind her smelling like my sandalwood body wash.

Finding the space heater takes a little more work. I finally locate it in the top of the hall closet and quickly work to plug it in before double-checking the water temperature. Then I slip back out to the living area where Jett has once again sunk into a blanket cocoon with only the top of her head peeking out. I softly massage what I can reach before telling her the shower is ready. Once she disappears down the hall and I hear the door latch, I head into the kitchen to throw together a small lunch. I only got toast into Jett's stomach earlier. She needs to eat.

By the time the water shuts off, a tray of fruit, BLTs, a water for me and a Dr. Pepper for Jett sit on the coffee table by the love seat. As Jett slips back into the room, I motion toward the cushions on the floor for her where it'll be easier for me to brush her hair, but she walks straight to me, the black sweats I'd left in the bathroom for her swallowing her petite frame. Without thought, I open my arms and envelop her.

"You said don't ask. Just do."

"I did."

"Thank you."

Without another word, I lead Jett to her spot and sit behind her, her body fitting perfectly between my knees as I carefully comb the tangles from her hair.

After spending fifteen minutes blow drying her hair, I sit back to brush out any new tangles. Several moments in, I have to double check that Jett is still awake. Her body keeps going lax against my leg or the front of the love seat, and she never makes a peep. Finally, as I am attempting to braid her hair—something I haven't tried to do since my sister was a kid—Jett speaks and, funnily enough, brings up my sister.

"I mean, who has girly bath stuff in their manly bathroom?"

I chuckle. "Oakley leaves her stuff here for when she drops in between flights out of Atlanta, like the night you met her.

She'll swing by long enough for a shower and some sleep then she's gone again."

Jett is thoughtful for a moment before she says, "You should talk about them more. Your family, I mean. I know the sad. I want to know the good, too."

"Yeah?"

At her drowsy nod, I start to explain, but a knock at the door halts the conversation.

"To be continued," I mumble against her crown before leaving another kiss and standing to open the door, knowing it is McKenna. "Get comfy on the couch, love. I'll let Sadie back in to snuggle you."

McKenna took one look at Jett before taking control of the situation. Though I don't actually know what the situation is. I tried to leave the girls with their privacy, but my loft is only so large. Even Sadie has made herself at home with Jett. I swear that dog loves her more than she loves me.

After what seems like forever, McKenna brings the now-empty food tray back into the kitchen where I've been watching videos on some new elevator models.

"Did she tell you what happened yesterday?" I ask McKenna, doubting I'll get a straightforward answer.

"You'll have to ask her. Best friend confidentiality and all." She turns from the sink of dirty dishes and looks at me, face somber. "Look, that girl has been through hell and back more than once. She's the kind of girl who can sit at rock bottom for weeks before you will notice. Her heart is usually the culprit, so it's not something to toy with. If you are just here for a quick venture to her bedroom, or if she is your next fix for the next little stretch of time, then leave her alone. Do not try to comfort her. Do not tell her it will all be okay. Do not pass 'GO,' and do not collect two hundred dollars."

I shake my head at McKenna. "I'm not goin' anywhere, Kenna. That girl means something. More than something. She's supposed to be in my life." I pause, looking back toward the couch where my personal bundle of chaos is curled up with Sadie, eyes unfocused as she stares toward the television, hand absentmindedly stroking the Aussie's coat. "She is all that matters to me. I just want her happy." It must be the right thing to say, because McKenna's lips tip into a grin.

"A few years ago, you would have been out that door without a second thought."

"Four months ago, I wouldn't have taken off work just to look after someone." I shrug. Her words are not wrong. Back when I'd met McKenna, I'd been a young twenty-something guy looking to get lucky. She'd been witness to it, watching me fly through partners. Now, though? Now I only have eyes for the kind of chaos that is Jett Taylor. "Like I said, this means something. Jett isn't just some hookup."

"You don't need to explain it to me, Noah. I know how special she is. She and her brother both." Her words draw my focus, making me really *look* at McKenna and think back to how we met.

"I know you wanted out from under Trace's thumb back in the day because you fell for someone less toxic. It was because of Reece, wasn't it?"

She shoves my shoulder gently before laughing softly at my reddening cheeks and passing me the empty fruit bowl to refill, fully evading my question. "Just go be with her. Let her snuggle you under all the blankets. Feed her fruit and cookies. Fund her Dr. Pepper addiction. All she really needs is someone who will listen, both to what she says and what she keeps to herself."

I nod at McKenna as she lets herself out then I make my way over to only girl to ever make me feel like this. How does a guy like me deserve the chance to be with a woman like this?

***

"You ready to talk about yesterday?" I ask as I slip under the blankets and pull Jett's legs into my lap, scooting closer to her.

The only indication that she hears me is a slight lift and drop of the blankets covering most of Jett's body, including her head. Letting my hands roam up and down her legs, I sit quietly while watching the halftime report. We usually fast forward through it, but it seems like a good excuse to talk today.

Choosing my words carefully, I ask, "What happened yesterday, sweet girl?"

The blankets drop slightly, just enough for me to see that gorgeous face, perfect little button nose, and those amber-flaked green eyes.

"There she is." I pour as much adoration into my expression as I can, squeezing right above her knee as I watch her eyelids flutter.

"Keep doing that and words won't come," she warns quietly.

I offer a cheeky grin. "But you would."

The shade of red her face turns could give the red line on the ice a run for its money. "Not cool, Slater."

"In all seriousness, you look exceptionally cute peeking out of your blanket igloo."

"And you're full of shit."

Reaching a hand out, I push back a loose strand of hair. "No shit, you are more beautiful than you give yourself credit for. You far exceed any other woman I know. Now tell me what had you out of sorts yesterday."

The up tilt of her lips isn't a smile, but it is progress. "Joey—my ex. He texted me yesterday, and I didn't handle it well. Clearly. Jumped right into old habits I thought I'd knocked off years ago."

I force my hands to stay lax, but my heart rate picks up at the mention of a guy who had this perfect woman and gave her up.

"It wasn't even anything big. He just reached out to see how I was doing. Which is a very Joey-like thing. We were friends before we ever started dating, and he always wanted to make sure everyone in his life was okay, happy." Her hand finds mine under the blankets. "It's not whatever you're imagining right now. I don't miss our relationship—we needed to end—but it has taken hours of therapy sessions with Kristen to realize that I am stronger without Joey in my life. Sure, if we'd ended sooner, it wouldn't have been as painful. But he wasn't in love with me, and I was just comfortable with him. I can admit that now."

"So, how'd that result in your drunken escapade?"

She shrugs. "I overthought things. Realized it has been four months since everything started falling apart. Things between me and Reece are strained still. I'm trying to stand on my own two feet. Didn't want to bother you when I knew you hadn't gotten in until late Saturday."

"You keeping tabs on me, chaos?"

That shoulder tilt again. "I like knowing you're home before I go to sleep," she says bashfully. This girl.

At that, I lift the blankets off of us and pull Jett into my arms. I tuck the blankets back around the two of us before she can protest. "So, back to what you were saying. Did you text your ex back?"

"Not exactly. According to my call log, I dialed his number and his best friend before I went to Riley's. No clue what I said, but since they were both only minute long calls, it couldn't have been much. I keep waiting for one of them to call me back, but they haven't."

"Do you want them to?" I ask, waiting on bated breath. I won't sit back and let this loser have her. Not without a fight.

"A little. I promise it's not because I want to get back together. The only guy I want is here in Havenwood." She grins up at me, those emerald eyes cutting straight into my soul. "But I miss my friends, and I would like to think we'd be able to get back to some of that back if I can get past the hurt." She lets out a dry laugh. "Then again, can anyone get past finding their boyfriend getting it on with their friend in the living room after a long day at work?"

I play with the hand that she still has in mine, rubbing circles on her palm. "I think it depends on if you're both truly happy in your new situations. Would I like the girl I care about hanging with her cheating ex? Probably not, but I'd like to think I'm secure enough to accept it."

After a minute of silence, I ask, "You know my brother married your brother's ex while they were still supposedly in a relationship?"

"That...actually makes Reece's issues with you make a lot of sense."

"Apparently, I'm the only one who didn't know why until recently."

"It's a stupid reason. Some if it is also because you're an elevator mechanic and our dad always talked shit about you guys. Again. Stupid reason to not like the coolest guy in town."

I keep my gaze on the television but silently bask in the warmth her words provide. "Communication can go such a long way. Instead, idiots assume things and create easily avoidable and unnecessary confrontations. Anyway, the girl that Trace just split with was your brother's girl when she and Trace eloped." Shaking my head, I let myself squeeze Jett's thigh again, my fingers trailing up ever so gently.

"I convinced myself romance isn't real after the Joey and Ella thing. First, my parents split because it was just a marriage of convenience and Mom fell in love with her assistant. She and Jared have twin daughters who are pre-teens now."

"Do you get to see them often?"

"Not really. I struggle with a relationship with my mom. She had trouble understanding me as a teen anyway, and then when Dad moved to Kentucky after the split, it was and still is a rocky relationship. But her husband and my sisters are cool."

"Are you and your dad close?"

She smiles. "Oh yeah, he's the best. He doesn't get to come down from Kentucky often, but we talk on the phone all the time."

I lean down to kiss her temple again, loving the feel of her in my arms. "Since we are telling each other *all the things* as you like to say, you promised talk of a first date."

A groan slips through her lips that makes me smile. "I did, didn't I?"

"Tell me what's off-limits. I don't want to go planning something that'll ruin a chance at a second date."

She sits quietly for a moment before slowly nodding her head. "Crowded places are a big no for me when I can help it. Um, I prefer places I know, too."

"Do you have any aversions to going somewhere by hiking or horseback?"

"No, not really. It's been a hot minute since I rode anything, though." When she looks at me with a soft blush seeping up her neck at the sexual inuendo she accidentally let slip, I can't help but lean forward and touch my lips to her temple.

"Okay, new topic. How's the freelancing going? Still have clients pouring in?"

She snorts before giggling at herself. The lightness to her features, her mood elevated, brings my heartrate up. It takes everything in me not to kiss the chaos before me.

"Hilarious. Pouring in. More like trickling as slow as molasses. I had three clients follow me, but their next big projects are still a few months away."

"You can always work as a farmhand. Declan could use someone to groom and tack horses for him while Drew is still getting his strength back."

Jett shakes her head but leans closer into me, snuggling into my side. "I can't be that close to Reece all day, every day. We'll strangle each other with baling twine." Her ill-placed humor has her giggling again, and it's the best sound I've heard in years. Making Jett Taylor laugh is one of my new goals in life.

"I asked around about making your dream come to fruition."

"You mean the one that's meant to stay a dream?" Shaking her head again, she huffs a breath before leaning back against the couch, eyes closing. "I've asked around. I've checked the board at the bar. There aren't any commercial lease locations available."

Reaching back to squeeze my neck and hoping like hell I'm not overstepping, I say, "I talked to Kelsey. She's interested in giving you a starting place at the bakery. She has that whole extra room that is just sitting space. You could create a mini bookstore set-up and offer your freelancing out of there, too, if you had clients that wanted to meet in person."

Her eyes pop open, studying me. There's a mix of embarrassment and what looks like awe on her face. "You've really thought this through, haven't you?"

"One of these days, you'll believe that I'm in this for the long haul with you. I want you to succeed and to be happy." I bring my hand up to grasp her jaw. "Don't you dare shake that pretty head of yours 'no' one more time tonight, sweet girl. You are capable. You *can* make your dream a reality, and this entire town will support you."

Jett's eyes get misty, but she blinks it back. "Well, when you put it like that." She sniffs and takes a deep breath, holds it for a few seconds then breathes out slowly. "Why are you so perfect, Noah Slater?"

"Not perfect," I say. "We just seem to balance each other."

"Like order and chaos."

"Like order and chaos.

My favorite smile graces her lips, the softest look in her eyes as she whispers, "Perfect."

CHAPTER TWENTY-THREE

Noah

> Noah: I need ideas. Romantic ideas.

McKenna: Please tell me this is for our girl.

> Noah: Duh. Who else?

Kelsey: AHHH! She told me she said yes to a date :)

McKenna: Blankets. Legos. Dr. Pepper. Blankets.

Noah: What do I do with that, Monroe?

Kelsey: You can do a book bouquet! Or are y'all going out?

McKenna: She'd be happy curling up on the couch. Nowhere busy. Keep to her comfort zones.

Kelsey: She wants you to read her spicy books.

Noah: How do you know that?

Kelsey: I don't, but it'd be sexy. Right, McKenna?

Kelsey: We need to meet. You'd like me, I swear.

Noah: *face palm*

McKenna: I've got your number now. Next time I visit.

McKenna: And yes. Sexy as hell, but will embarrass her.

Noah: Ladies, you still haven't told me what to do.

McKenna: Not going to. You know what she likes. You're overthinking this big time.

Noah: *eye roll*

Kelsey: Stop with the emojis. She's right, Mr. Grumpy.

Noah: *thumbs up*

"If we blow this whole dating thing up, just remember that I told you not to waste your time with me."

Rolling my eyes as we walk across the street to the bakery, I tuck her tighter into my side. "I know that. Actually, your exact words back in January were 'hot mess central.'"

"Please save me from repeating my own words. I know what I said. I still believe it all, but I don't need to hear it repeated back to me. No need to mock me."

"Never, baby girl. I just wanted to remind you that you. Are. Wrong. You are a beaut' inside and out—hot mess and all—and I want nothing more than to take you out—or in—if you'll really let me. We can go to dinner, we can have a picnic, or we can hide out in one of our apartments and order takeout. Whatever scenario will get you to date me, I'll gladly accept."

I'm a relationship guy, through and through. I did the *hit 'em and quit 'em* thing in high school and my early twenties and realized pretty quick that it wasn't for me. Most women don't want to stay trapped in such a small town. Then the one relationship I thought might have a chance was ripped away before we had the opportunity to try. Jett is the first girl who's made me want to give a serious relationship another chance. As I tell her all of this, she stares at me, wide-eyed.

Chuckling, I say, "Crazy right? How could anyone hate living here? Everyone always in your business. One bank, one diner-slash-bar, one bakery, one miniscule grocery store and package store."

"And yet you love it."

"Don't you? This place is a community. A family. If I needed a place to stay, ten people would offer a roof. If I needed groceries, I'd have meals delivered to last for days. That's just how the people in this town are, and I absolutely love it. There is nowhere I would rather grow old. Hopefully raise some kiddos and teach them the same respect that this place taught me."

"You want kids?"

"Not a deal breaker, but I can see little ones running around. Not in the loft, but there's a rental of mine that I'd like to move

into, eventually. The view out the back window is phenomenal. Plenty of yard for dogs or kids."

"You have it all planned out, huh?"

Opening the door to the sweet smell of baked goods and
coffee, Isay, "Sweet girl, if I told you every thought going
through my head about the future, you'd have tucked tail and
run before I ever got you out the door earlier."

"Probably."

"Not probably. I guarantee it, chaos."

She's quiet for a minute, staring at the display case, then says,
"I think I want two kids. Close in age. I always said if I didn't
have kids by the time that I was thirty, then I wouldn't have
kids, but I think with the right guy I'd throw that out." Her
eyes cut to me for a breath before she tells the high schooler
behind the counter what she wants. Meanwhile, my heart is
soaring as I likely read too deep into that singular look.

***

The mid-March air has a bite to it this year.

With Georgia, you never know what you might get, weath-
er-wise. It could be forty-eight degrees and overcast in the
morning and seventy-eight that afternoon with a good chance
of too much sun. This morning, I pick up Jett—meaning I
wait for her to get ready and meet her at our doors—and we

make our way to Kelsey's Café across the way. It has become somewhat of a routine, much like our Sunday afternoons. Now, Friday mornings are ours, too, since I work four tens and she's started helping out in the café a few late mornings each week.

We walk shoulder-to-shoulder, which is really more like her head to my shoulder, and slip into the warmth of the bakery. "Go ahead and order whatever you want. I'm going to go find Kels real quick."

Jett looks questioningly at me but nods. She immediately steps up to the counter, ordering both of our regular coffee orders while I slip around the corner toward the back office in search of Kelsey.

I find her behind her desk, phone to her ear in a hushed conversation. I knock on the door frame, and she looks up, startled. As she realizes it's me, her voice quickens.

"Gotta go. I'll call you later, hun." She quickly ends the call, storing her cell phone in her pocket.

"Everything okay, Kels?"

"Yeah." She nods then shakes her head. "Just some crazy inventory issues that I was trying to work out with one of the early morning gals. What can I do ya for?"

Even though I'm more than used to Kelsey's antics, I find myself tilting my head. "You're hiding something," I mutter, crossing my arms over my chest and leaning against the door frame.

She grins, mischief in her eyes. I can't stop the answering grin on my face before shaking my head and rolling with it. Kelsey is her own being and there is no understanding how she works. I know better than to ask what she's hiding.

"That business plan we discussed. You still in?" I ask her,leaning my head out into the hallway to look for Jett.

Kelsey's eyes light up in excitement. "You brought Jett? Have you told her I'm interested yet?"

Shaking my head, I look back across the room. "You're more excited than she is. Yes, I spoke with her about it. Seems like she's interested, too."

"I hope she goes for it."

"Goes for what? Who?" Jett asks as she slips under my arm, handing my double espresso Irish cream coffee to me before taking a sip of her iced caramel latte. She looks between me and Kelsey before walking closer to the desk and dropping into one of the padded chairs there. Kelsey sits up straighter, folding her hands together and leaning her head on them.

"I want you to open a bookstore. Here. In the back part of the café. It's not a huge space. Roughly twenty by thirty-two."

Jett looks to me, nibbling that lip. I can almost see her thoughts rolling off her. Can she succeed? She didn't think I was serious about talking to Kelsey for her. She doesn't think Kelsey is serious about this.

When Jett remains silent, lost in her thoughts, I step closer and rest a hand on her shoulder, my thumb grazing the skin at the top of her neck. "You said your dream was to open a bookstore in a small town and run your editing business out of it. Kelsey has the space in an already successful coffee shop."

"But how? When?" She lets out a huff of air as her legs start their nervous bouncing.

Kelsey leans forward, meeting Jett's eyes before glancing up at me and back to Jett. "Noah brought up that you wanted to run a bookstore but that there weren't any spaces to lease right now. I loved the idea. Have always had the idea, actually. And Spring Market is this weekend. What better time to announce that we are expanding?"

"You actually want to expand your business? With me?" Jett squeaks, complete surprise lining her voice. "But why?"

"Chaos, haven't you learned yet? This community is all about making dreams come true."

"We don't have to make any definite plans yet. We can just let people know it's coming soon, then move as fast or as slow as you want." Kelsey's eyes gleam with excitement, the wheels already turning on how to make this happen as quickly as possible.

I look at Jett, hoping we aren't overstepping. "I know you wanted to do this all on your own, but sometimes a helping hand is a good thing."

She shakes her head. "No, I'm thankful for the help. Really. I'm just trying to wrap my head around it." She looks back to Kelsey and breaths deep. "I have a business plan somewhat pieced together, if you want to take a look? Obviously, components can be moved around since it's your business—"

"Our business," Kelsey interrupts. "We do this together. I mean, the café doesn't technically even have a name, so we strip things down as much as we need to make this exactly what both of us want."

A light sparks in Jett's eye, and a tension I hadn't noticed seeps from her shoulders, leaving her looking pounds lighter. "Well, if we really want to talk about name changes, I do have an idea. Feel free to say no." She slips her phone from her pocket and messes around for a second before asking Kelsey for her email. "Okay, you should have it in your inbox."

I step closer to Jett, resting my hand on her lower back, my thumb rubbing along her spine. She glances up at me and mouths *thank you* before Kelsey's squeal of excitement startles us both.

"You like it?" Jett asks tentatively.

Kelsey shakes her head. "I love it, Jett." She holds a hand out to shake. As Jett joins in, Kelsey pulls her close into a hug. "Welcome to the future home of The Write Brew, Jett."

CHAPTER TWENTY-FOUR

Jett

"Did Kelsey convince you to come to Spring Market this weekend?"

I nod at Jace's question while nibbling my lip. "I've been told that it's a rite of passage for becoming a citizen of this town. So, it sounds like I might not really have a choice." Picking up a fry and pointing it at him, I continue. "Although I have to say—I am not excited about being thrown into the deep end with the entire town's population."

Jace nods along as he dries off the glasses he just washed. The bar is exceptionally quiet today, especially for a Thursday evening, but I don't mind. It means I don't feel quite so uptight. And since I promised Noah I would do my best not to drink away my problems after last weekend's fiasco, Jace is supplying me with soda and french fries until I get bored and decide to go home. Probably not going to happen any time soon, since I have my Kindle out and am reading a steamy cowboy romance where the rancher has his girl up against the side of the barn.

A hand on my shoulder has me jumping straight out of my skin, my tablet tumbling to the short counter behind the bar. When I look up from where it landed—luckily out of any liquids—Kelsey is standing there, her hands raised in defense, eyes wide in shock.

"Sorry," I mutter.

"I did *not* mean to make you do that. I said your name a few times, but you were in your own world," she says apologetically.

I shake my head. "Not your fault. You know I get lost in here," I say, tapping my temple to indicate my brain.

"Ooh, which one are you reading now? Is it spicy?"

We realized the other day during our discussion of our new business venture that we share a love of romance novels. I know my cheeks are red at her question; I've always gotten embarrassed when people ask what I am reading. I know I shouldn't. Everyone is entitled to enjoy what they enjoy, regardless of the content.

As Kelsey slips behind the bar, retrieving my tablet for me, she glances at the screen. "Oh man, I've been wanting to read that! How is it?" she asks as she realizes it is Bailey Hannah's debut novel.

"It's really good. Austin is most definitely book boyfriend material." I leave out any details, because I always hate when people spoil things for me. It could be some minor detail, but it is a detail I want to learn organically. And the trauma of the female main character should definitely be read without outside influence.

I also keep to myself that Austin is not who I picture in that barn scene. Heh. Not internal me fanning myself as I picture Noah Slater holding me against the barn up the road and whispering dirty things in my ear.

"Earth to Jett," Kelsey says as she taps the counter in front of me with a beer glass.

As my eyes snap up to hers, she smiles. Always smiles on this woman, I swear.

"Lost you for a few minutes there. Thinking about anything worth sharing?"

And the blush is back. Damn. I shake my head no, but the corner of my lips tips up. "Nothing that would not embarrass us both if I voiced it. Especially with guys working here tonight."

"Might you be fantasizing about a certain dark-haired, dark-eyed mechanic?"

"Shhh." I almost throw my tablet back across the bar but settle for swatting innocently at her arm. Surely, everyone in this place can now see how red my face is.

"Oh, honey. No need to be embarrassed. We all know you two are together. Heck, Noah has flat out declared that you are off-limits to any other guy in Havenwood."

"I'm sorry. What?" Surely, I heard her incorrectly.

"Don't you give me that crap, Jett Taylor. That man is so smitten with you that I could strip in front of him and he wouldn't even blink in my direction, because he only has eyes for you. Tell me you are not that dense."

Flustered, I try to sift through my whirling thoughts. "We've been spending time together," I say, wringing my hands in my lap now. "I may or may not have gone to meet his family a few weeks ago."

The shattering of a glass has me and Kelsey glancing toward the other end of the bar, where Jace is cursing under his breath as he sweeps up the shards.

I cringe as I realize he was eavesdropping. "Going out on a limb and guessing Noah didn't tell Jace about it."

"Sometimes my twin likes to overstep," she hollers over her shoulder, intentionally letting Jace hear before looking back at me. "Sometimes, Jace can be a little overbearing where his family is concerned. And Noah is definitely family. So are you, ya know."

Jace slips back through the kitchen entrance and slides a plate of chicken fingers with a side of ranch in front of me.

"Your boyfriend said to feed you real food. Something about you getting too distracted to eat lately."

I roll my eyes. "He's such a worry wart." And yet, I still dig into the food, because he's right. I may or may not get too distracted to remember to fix three meals a day. Kelsey's knowing smile draws a blush to my face, but I change the subject.

"So, Spring Market," I say between bites of fried goodness. "What exactly am I supposed to expect aside from way too many people in too small of an area?"

Jace chuckles, but Kelsey shoots me a sympathetic glance. She may be the most over joyous individual I have ever met, but she also understands me about as well as McKenna always has. She is quickly worming her way into my—very tiny—circle of trust.

"It really isn't that bad," she offers, as if she is trying to excuse the town from something. It just seems like she thinks the town itself is why I am struggling with the idea of going. And maybe it is.

"I don't do crowds."

"We know," the twins say in unison.

Usually, a response like that toward one of my quirks would set me on edge. And yet, with these guys—much like with

Noah—I don't feel a need to defend myself or offer excuses. They know I struggle with daily tasks that put me around new people. They know I zone out, but they don't get irritated with me when it happens. They know to be direct if they want me to understand something the first time around.

It is in this moment I realize Jace is right there with Kelsey in slipping behind the iron-clad walls I have built around my heart.

My eyes dart left as I try to wrangle the sudden bubble of emotion settling in my chest. After a moment, I take a staggered breath and start the conversation back up.

"I just need a breakdown of what to expect. Events, when to be where, where to avoid. All the things."

Jace steps away to tend to a few patrons that have slipped in, so Kelsey answers me. "Everything kicks off at ten. Booths from all the shops in town followed by a chili-making contest. Buck's deer chili almost always wins. Then at three, fun events start happening down at the Flynn's place. There is a fun jackpot-style barrel race that's mostly teenagers. Then we hook up the four wheelers to sleds, wet down the arena, and see who can hold on the longest."

My eyes widen as I try to imagine what she is describing. "That sounds more than a little dangerous."

"Oh, it is. But it is so much fun. So freeing."

"You have fun with that." I laugh. The things small town people do for fun.

CHAPTER TWENTY-FIVE

Jett

McKenna: So?

Jett: So, what?

McKenna: Are you guys dating?

Kelsey: Oh, so dating. So CUTE, too!

Jett: What? No!

Kelsey: That's why he kissed your fore-head this morning.

Oakley: Too early for gross texts about my brother.

Oakley has left the chat
Kelsey has added Oakley to the chat

Kelsey: Sorry, Oaks. They are just too precious.

Jett: Ok can we not? You're embarrassing me.

McKenna: *evil laugh* I love having backup.

Jett: Someone else find a lover so y'all can leave me alone.

Oakley: My guess is Kelsey.

Kelsey: *side-eye emoji*

Kelsey: Not me. BUT I have it on good authority...Leila is moving back to town.

Oakley: Wait...NO!! Does Drew know?

Kelsey: Oops. Forgot you knew that story. Keep this to yourself.

"That logo is badass," McKenna says as she walks over, her blue eyes fixed on the banner Noah and Jace just finished securing for me. A local teen designed the *Coming Soon* banner with The Write Brew's new logo for us to hang on the front of the café so everyone coming through would see it.

Pulling her into a hug, I can't stop the pride from bubbling up inside.

"You're doing it, babe," she whispers into my hair.

I squeeze her tighter to me, knowing she's part of the reason I've made it this far but not being able to voice the words. As we step apart, I bring her into the conversation with Noah and Kelsey.

"Kels, I know Noah does, but do you know McKenna?"

McKenna reaches out a hand, but Kelsey won't have it and launches at my oldest friend, wrapping her into a hug.

"McKenna Monroe! You're a legend." As she takes a step back, she has the decency to apologize, embarrassment marring her cheeks. "It's just, I've followed your workouts for years. Naughty Peach Athletics is the only program I've ever stuck with."

I clear my throat as McKenna's face pales, and Noah takes a step back. "Someone want to fill me in on what I'm missing?"

McKenna tries to force a laugh, unable to meet my eyes.

Kelsey, nearly as bad as me at reading the room, speaks up. "Only the hottest dirty workout on the internet."

"It's not dirty," McKenna bursts. "It's about loving your body and being comfortable in your skin."

"I think I'm going to slip over to talk to Declan while you ladies discuss this," Noah says before dropping a kiss to the top of my head.

I start to protest, but he holds his hands up and backs away.

"Yes, I knew. You can fuss at me later."

Glancing back at the girls, I say, "You mean my best friend is a badass athletic instructor and no one bothered to tell me?"

"She is. You *need* to look up one of the workouts," Kelsey gushes. I've never seen the girl so out of sorts, and it is honestly amusing. McKenna's cheeks are taking on a pink hue as mortification eases into embarrassment.

"It's not exactly mainstream. And, clearly, I don't advertise to people I know."

Before I can question her for more details, Drew walks up. It's good to see him out of his braces and not looking like he's in pain.

"Hey, Jett? Some dude is asking for you. I didn't tell him where you were, but he seemed adamant that he talks to you. Said he stopped by your brother's house and was told you'd be here. I tried to call Reece to confirm, but he isn't answering. He's up at the ranch's booth," he says before turning and walking back to the middle of the town square where all the tents for Spring Market are set up.

I share glances with the girls. There's only one guy who would come looking for me. I try to pick through the crowd, suddenly wanting Noah close but unable to see him.

"Joey?" McKenna asks.

"Gotta be, right? Anyone see where Noah went?"

Kelsey suddenly looks ready to attack. "Wait. The cheating ex is here? Where? Let me at him!"

Despite the growing knot in my stomach, I find a smidge of amusement in the enthusiasm of my pint-sized friend. "If someone sees Noah, can you send him searching for me, please?"

With that, I wander toward Drew's booth. As I round the corner of the tent, my feet cement themselves to the ground, breath catching completely in my chest. Because I come face-to-face with an impeccably dressed man who so clearly does not belong in Havenwood.

"Joey."

The protective walls around my heart and mind that had been slowly crumbling since moving here immediately snap back into place as if there had never been any give in their structure.

Because the person responsible for the creation of those walls is standing before me.

As he always did, Joey reads my face before I utter a word. His hands come up defensively, as if ready to block a blow. "Before you walk away—which you have every right to do—your brother is the one that told me I could find you here."

I am going to strangle Reece. I'm sure there's plenty of baling twine around here. Maybe Drew will help me. I force a breath of air into my lungs and count to five before breathing out and demanding my body not react. Emotions have left the building, y'all.

"Why are you here, Joey?"

"Can we possibly go sit and talk? Away from prying ears?"

I cut my eyes to where he is looking and see both Flynn brothers watching intently from a fairly short distance away. And for once, I'm thankful for small town gossip. Hopefully someone will send Noah this direction soon.

"The whole town will know anything we say by the end of the night. It's how this place works."

"Illusion, Jett. Please, can we talk somewhere quieter?"

A weighted sigh slips out, but I lead Joey off the square, heading toward the back entrance of the café while keeping quiet the whole walk over. Once we are inside and the door is firmly closed, I lean against it.

"What the hell are you doing here, Joey?" I demand, emotions I'd rather not have surface bubbling toward the top. I've just started getting into the swing of things with Noah. I do not need this right now.

Joey at least has the decency to look sheepish, rubbing the back of his neck without looking at me for a minute or two. "You told me to give you some time, but I wanted—no, *needed*—to check on you. Your call a few weeks ago had me worried. And then you wouldn't answer my texts or calls, so I reached out to your brother instead. He said if I wanted to apologize, I could come here, but that if I wanted anything else that I wasn't welcome in Havenwood, ever." He shakes his head. "I know I hurt you. And I'm sorry. I miss you, Jett."

"You don't get that luxury. Or burden, I guess. Depends on how you look at it."

A slight tick in his jaw is the only indication of his irritation. "We spent years loving each other. I didn't just quit caring about you."

"And you threw it away. Regardless of where we were in our relationship, whether it was falling apart or already over. You cheated on me in my own home."

He nods. "And I will never be able to apologize enough for not telling you when I first I realized what I was feeling for Ella."

I hop onto the counter, my back firmly pressed to the cabinet door. "I want to hate you."

"You have every right to."

"I know. But I don't."

He looks at me quizzically, like he doesn't believe me.

"I'm finally finding my happy. And yeah, it is a shitty way to get there, but if things hadn't ended between us when they did, I don't know if I would have ever moved here." Taking a deep breath, I find my feet again and stand taller in front of the man who made me feel unworthy of love. "I moved here because I couldn't bear living between the same walls that you and I had shared. But doing that? I've made friends with people that just roll with the punches when I don't make sense. They make sure to be direct if they need something. Moving here is the best decision I've made for myself."

As the words pour out, I realize how true they are. I'm learning to stand up for myself, that my worth isn't tied into anyone else's ideals.

"Drew—the guy that came to get me just now—he's been through hell but still steps up for those around him. Kelsey can keep up with my thoughts better than I can and is helping me put the business plan that you laughed at into action. Jace encourages me to be social in an environment that won't push my comfort zone too much. And McKenna comes down when she can." Unexpected tears burn the backs of my eyes as the realization hits me. "They all get me. This whole town has been my saving grace. A safe haven."

"You're thriving here."

"Noah is a big part of that."

"Noah?"

"My, well, he's not officially my boyfriend—like, we haven't labeled it or anything—but he gets me. Watches hockey with me, quiets my mind with just a touch. He's teaching me how to see my own worth."

"You love him."

I nod.

"You tell him yet?"

I shake my head this time.

The door to the back room opens with Noah storming in like a hurricane.

"Chaos? You okay? Drew said you left and..." His words trail off as he takes in Joey standing across from me. Noah easily reads the room and quickly slides closer to me, wrapping me tightly in his arms and kissing the top of my head. "You good?"

I nod.

"Chaos?" Joey asks.

Nodding again, I force my attention back to Joey, even though all I want to do is melt into my mechanic. "He's called me that pretty much since I met him."

"And you let him?" he asks, flabbergasted.

It's like I'm a dang bobble head with all the nodding I'm doing.

"He could call me just about anything, and I would let him." I love my Noah. I relax into his hold, but he shifts me slightly to extend his hand to Joey.

"Noah Slater."

"Joey Sanchez."

"You tore my girl's self-confidence up."

Joey nods once, not taking his eyes off of my significant other. Probably for the best. I can feel the coiling of Noah's muscles as he finally puts a face to the heartache he had to fight through so hard.

"If I remember correctly, and I'm certain that I do because my memory is excellent, I'm pretty sure you told my girl that she was a lot to handle when, in fact, she doesn't need any kind of handling. She's perfect all on her own."

Joey looks between me and Noah before his gaze settles back on me. "I won't pretend to be innocent."

"Well, that's a relief," I say.

"You grew a backbone."

"It's amazing what happens when you quit letting other people dictate your life."

"I'll get out of your hair. After your call and then not hearing back from you, I just needed to make sure you were okay."

"Real worried, huh? That call was a month ago."

"She has everything she needs," Noah says, a slight growl to his tone that has a giggle threatening to bubble out of me. I've never had a guy get growly over me.

Joey starts for the door but pauses as he opens it to step out. "Keep chasing your happy, Jett. You deserve it." And with that, he's gone.

I turn into Noah's chest, burying my face in the base of his neck. His fingers gingerly stroke my head, playing with my hair. A deep sigh bordering on a groan escapes my throat as he adds a little more pressure, making my knees weak as the swirling thoughts freeze.

"Love you," I mumble drowsily.

It isn't until his hand stops and I feel more than hear his breathing pause that I realize what just slipped out.

Old Jett would back away and run. Go for a walk. Avoid.

Chase your happy.

Embrace the chaos.

Stepping back just a smidgen, I look up at Noah, my arms settling on his waste. "I love you, Noah. I think you already know that, but I need to vocalize it. I love you. I love you. I love you."

His hand trails up to my jaw, cupping my cheek and running a thumb over my lips. "Best sound I've ever heard is those words coming from these lips," he whispers before leaning down and capturing my lips into the gentlest of kisses. He pulls back just enough to add, "I love you too, Jett Taylor," before pulling me close and swaying us side to side.

We stay like that, just enjoying being held by each other, until a thought about the way Noah addressed Joey breaks through my daze.

"So, you're a growly man now, huh? Trying to imitate my book beaus?"

The full belly laugh that escapes Noah is contagious, and before we know it, both of us are fanning the flame between us while trying not to combust.

"If we don't stop now, we aren't making it back down to the festivities." Glancing at the little microwave for the time, he continues. "We have less than twenty minutes to get over to the ranch before someone comes looking for us."

"I don't care," I groan, going up on tiptoes to try reaching his lips again.

Noah chuckles, obviously enjoying my irritation. "I don't think scarring your brother or our friends should be on your to-do list today, sweet girl."

"No fun." Noah keeps that smirk on his face until I add, "I'm kidding. Kind of."

"My girl's got jokes today," he says before leaning down to drop a kiss on my waiting lips.

I can't help but smile up at him, my hands reaching for his belt. Before I can touch the buckle, both hands are swept into one of his large ones behind my back, effectively containing me.

"Be good, and I promise to make it worth your while when we get home."

Those words shoot straight to my core as a whimper slips from my lips.

"Deal?" he asks, his breath hot on my neck.

I nod, but it's not enough for him.

With a nip below my ear, he mumbles, "Words, pretty girl. Do we have a deal?"

"Yes," I squeak.

"That's my girl." He steps back, releases my hands, and is at the door before my mind has caught up with what just happened.

Chapter Twenty-Six

Jett

Sometimes, sinking into a mountain of pillows with a weighted blanket on my lap, the *Hamilton* soundtrack playing softly, and a big fluffball of a dog curled into my side is exactly what I need to be productive. I'm in the zone, flying through edits on the sweetest client's first manuscript. It's all going so well, until a gentle hand lands on my shoulder and squeezes.

"What the hell, Noah? I was in the middle of something." I slam my laptop closed, my heart pounding in my ears. With my hyperfocus broken, I feel discombobulated. Like I was in an entirely different plane of existence and have been doused in ice-cold water.

As I jump to my feet, intent on storming off to—I don't know, somewhere—Noah grasps my fingers, spinning me into his chest and wrapping his arms snuggly around me.

Completely.

One arm is tightly holding the entirety of my waist while the other travels from hip to head, grazing his fingertips with just enough pressure. His lips rest at the crown of my head. I fight a little to get out of his hold, but he holds tighter.

"Breathe, gorgeous." His thumbs begin moving in tandem, taking gentle swipes along the skin that they can reach. One on my hip bone and the other on the base of my neck. "I didn't mean to break your focus, sweet girl."

I slowly relax against his chest, letting his body heat envelope me as my heart rate returns to normal. Turning my head, I rest my ear over his heart, letting the slow and steady rhythm soothe my own hummingbird heartbeat.

We stand in silence until my body sags against his completely.

"Sorry," I mumble into his shirt, the embarrassment of snapping at him for no logical reason hanging over me. My cheeks burn with it.

Noah slides his arm from my waist, bringing his hand up to gently grasp my chin between his fingers, effectively forcing my eyes up to his.

"What's going through that pretty head of yours?" he asks softly.

I test his grip by trying to turn my gaze away again, but he holds firm. Not hurting, but steady. A rock in the midst of my storm.

"I was trying to finish up some edits for this indie author's debut novel. I promised her that she'd have it back by tomorrow, but I keep getting distracted. I was finally in the groove. And we are creeping up on opening day for my dream store. It's literally less than three weeks away." Rubbing my eyes with the palms of my hands all while he still cradles my face, waiting patiently, I sigh again. "I lost track of time, I guess. And then you were suddenly just standing there, and it scared me."

Never have I ever had someone maintain this much eye contact when discussing something so minor. Not until Noah.

And when he grins? Holy fireballs, this guy.

As his lips meet mine, I am thankful his other arm is still holding me. This man.

Pulling away, he says, "Skin's a little flushed there, gorgeous. Feeling alright?" That grin still presses on his lips, a knowing glint in his eyes.

"No fair," I mumble, tucking my chin to my chest to avoid his gaze.

He walks me backward oh so slowly, until my back touches the wall. "Isn't it, though?" His fingers skim my skin, traveling from hip to breast to collarbone to neck. Calloused fingers grazing the column of my neck as he leans even closer.

"How?" I murmur, not really caring about the answer so long as he keeps doing what he's doing. As he steps closer, closing the space between our hips, I can feel how glad he is to be there.

"Because just looking at you, all nerdy innocence, has me wanting to touch. To taste. To claim."

I can't help myself; I rock into him just enough as his lips run a path along the shell of my ear. I whimper, need heating my body.

"Tell me what you need, Jett."

I want to tell him that I need him. That I want him to sink into me, make me forget everything that's gone wrong over the last few months. The last few years.

But what if that isn't what he is eluding to? What if I am reading all of this wrong? What if he doesn't like what I suggest?

What if, what if, what if?

My thoughts whirl together, none of them leaving my mouth, as if words are too difficult to form.

Increased pressure on the column of my neck short-circuits my thoughts as breathing becoming slightly more difficult. Suddenly, all thoughts stop.

Except one.

That dang whimper escapes again, and I can feel the grin against my skin before he pulls away slightly.

"Say that thought out loud for me, chaos. I can see it in your eyes," Noah says, his nose nearly grazing my own but not quite touching.

With hooded eyes and a shuddered breath, I whimper. "Need you." I roll my hips into his again, begging.

"Stay with me, chaos. The second I realize you're drifting, everything stops, yeah?"

A hum in my throat is my only acknowledgment as I search for contact. As pressure remains on my neck, his other hand slides down to my waist, finding and undoing the knot in the string of my sweatpants before slipping his hand inside, just avoiding the part of me that wants him most.

"Noah, please."

My hands reach for his waistband, but he stops me, removing his hands from me entirely. Crying at the loss of contact seems extreme, but my body is so tightly wound I don't know how to react.

"I've got you, baby." His arms reach down, hooking under my plaid-covered ass and lifting. "Just moving us somewhere more comfortable."

He carries me to the bedroom, tossing me onto the comforter like I'm nothing more than a rag doll. His thinner frame is misleading—the man is loaded in lean muscle. "Slide back and slip off those pants for me."

"Can you hit the lights?"

"I can, but I would rather you trust me enough to leave them on."

"It's just that—"

"Remember what happens if your mind starts to drift."

I snap my mouth closed.

"Do you trust me?"

Nodding, I chew on my lower lip. Unsure of how to act or what to say. Noah and I have discussed it before, but we have never played to his dominant side, because I have not been willing to trust him in the bedroom.

Make-out sessions and heavy petting? Sure.

Naked snuggles at bedtime? Absolutely.

But we have not gone this far. Hell, I wasn't sure I wanted to until a few days ago. I'd started to think that I would never crave this type of intimacy. Wondered if that part of me was irreparably damaged.

But baring myself under the LED lights for our first time? As someone who will not wear a bathing suit without a shirt over it... What if he regrets...damn it...

At some point, my eyes slip closed. I keep them squeezed tight as the bed dips, Noah's body caging me in from above.

"Keep your eyes closed, pretty girl. If you want me to stop at any point, just say so. Got me?"

My head gives a jerky nod, but I already know he wants verbal consent.

"Jett."

"Got you."

"Every part of you is perfection." Emotion threatens to choke me at his words, his touch. What did I do to deserve a man as perfect as him?

***

The sheets are rumpled and tucked around our naked bodies, our legs intertwined, my torso and head snuggled close to his chest. Those wide shoulders provide a sort of cocoon when his arms are wrapped around me.

Earlier today, Noah had come over with lunch, since it's a Sunday. He had wanted to watch a replay of the Voltage–Badgers playoff game from the day before. I'd already watched the game but love rewatching, so I'd recorded it. After we'd finished the recording, Noah said something about a shower and dinner, but I'd tuned it out as I was trying to finalize those edits. I'd forgotten he was even in the apartment until he'd startled me.

Noah's calloused hand traces lazy circles along my bare arm. "What's got you so tense, pretty girl?"

"I forgot you were here earlier," I whisper, still struggling to believe it. "I don't know that it was so much *forgot* as it was just not being on edge with someone in my space. Normally, I'm tense and wanting my weighted blankets until everyone is out of my hair. But I wasn't. I mean, I was under my blanket, but that was just because it was cozy."

His arms squeeze a little tighter in a hug before easing back up. "So, why'd you tense up when you realized that?" he asks.

"Because I wasn't expecting to get swallowed in emotional realizations shortly after sex."

His quiet laugh rumbles through his chest, his breath tickling my ear.

"Why are you laughing at me?"

"I'm not, I promise. You're adorable. All of you." He sighs as I tense up again, my back becoming rigid under his dutiful fingertips. "Help me out here, gorgeous."

"I feel like you're making fun of me."

"Never. You are perfect," he whispers into my ear with a kiss. "This. Whatever we are doing. Whatever you want us to be or not be. You need to communicate with me. Tell me what you want or what you don't like, yeah?"

"I've never been comfortable asking for what I want."

"Then you've been with the wrong kind of man. Tell me what you want. Always. If you don't like something. If you want me to do something else or try something different. I never want you to be afraid of me judging you for what you want. Everything you think, say, feel—it all matters. Remember that, yeah?" He runs his fingers through my hair, gently massaging my scalp as he goes, and I snuggle deeper into his side.

"Even if it's stupid?" I ask, feeling vulnerable.

"Have I ever made you feel that way, chaos?"

I shake my head. "I constantly feel like I'm waiting for the other shoe to drop with you. Like you're too good to be true. You're like this giant, lovable teddy bear disguised as a grizzly around everyone else, but I'm scared that I'm just seeing what I want. After Joey..." I trail off.

"I promise you I'm only into you. No other person has ever held my heart and soul like you do. I told you before. You are it for me."

"Your chaos?" I ask tentatively as he palms the back of my head and pulls me close.

"My bold, beautiful chaos."

CHAPTER TWENTY-SEVEN

Jett

"So, do you like this color scheme, or do you want to go brighter?" Kelsey asks.

My eyes flit from paint card to paint card as we sit in the front of the café. I can feel the anxiety building in my chest.

The grand opening of The Write Brew is right around the corner, and Kelsey has decided we need to repaint the café and the new book room—even though the guys already installed the bookshelves. Between serving customers and keeping the counter stocked, we have been moving non-stop.

"You already let me name it when it's mostly yours to begin with. I think you should pick the colors. I'm good with whatever. I swear," I say.

"My sweet, cautious Jett. You, my dear, need to live. This is *your* dream that we are bringing to life." The dreamy look on Kelsey's face puts a smile on mine. I never expected to find such a solid friendship when we started putting this plan into action, but I am beyond grateful. Even still, I shake my head, adamantly against claiming this dream as mine alone.

"It's your café, Kels. I'm just adding books."

"We are doing this together. You own half. Besides, I want to change things up... Tell you what. Your favorite color is purple, right?"

I nod, a little scared of where she's going with this, but also willing to let her ease some of the decision fatigue.

"Okay, so I'll just pick one of these that have the purple theme. How's that?"

"Whatever you want to do, Kels. Really. I'm so far out of my comfort zone here. Are we really three weeks out from the Summer Market already?"

The bell on the door chimes, and Noah slips in.

"Hi, gorgeous. What are you guys up to? Picking colors?

"Jett won't help me choose." Kelsey pokes out her lower lip in a ridiculous pout.

Noah hugs me closer and whispers, "Overwhelmed?"

I shrug noncommittally. While it may be true, I won't admit it. I want this place to be perfect. Can we make it what I've always dreamed of? A quiet, cozy escape from reality for the bookworm while also being a judgment-free zone for aspiring authors. With tasty treats and coffees and teas. Sandwiches during the lunch hour. The perfect getaway right in the town square.

Noah's warm hand settles over my lower back, his pinky dipping under my T-shirt as he brings my focus back to our current dilemma.

"When you thought about creating this place over the years, what colors were in your mind?"

"I don't know, Noah," I snap before I can stop myself. "The color doesn't matter. The atmosphere does."

His fingers slip around my hip and squeeze tight enough to grab my attention. It isn't as addictive as when he cradles my head, but it's a close second.

"Take a breath, chaos."

I work on centering myself. This isn't something to get out of sorts over. It's simple. I've fixated on it enough over the years.

"I always pictured dark wood and lavender with either olive or a deep teal."

Kelsey squeals. "That's perfect! I can take it from there if you want." She sashays to the back room that is now our shared office space.

"She driving you crazy yet?"

I pick up our empty mugs and carry them to the sink behind the counter and wash them so the two high schoolers working today won't have to. Although, my willingness to clean up has more to do with the pent-up energy that makes my skin tingle.

"I love her, but I think I need to go hide and decompress. When I walked through the door this morning, it was like she was waiting to pounce."

Noah snorts as he pulls me to the front of the café. "She probably was. That girl has been obsessed with this project since you agreed. Maybe even before that."

Reaching up on tiptoes, I brush a kiss across his lips, reveling in the feel as his arms wrap around me, his hands settling just above my ass.

"Can I steal you away for a bit?"

"Might be able to work something out. What for?"

Hugging me close, he drops a kiss to my temple. "I was hoping to convince you to just trust me and go along for the ride. I think you'll like it."

"Is there food?"

Nodding, he grins. "So, is your answer yes?"

"Whisk me away, Mr. Elevator Man."

***

And boy does he ever whisk me away.

"You know, this could be considered questionable behavior from a male suitor. Definitely morally gray behavior."

I can't see his face thanks to the blindfold he insisted I wear until we arrive wherever he's taking me, but his snort is perfectly audible and loaded with amusement.

"The number of book tropes that flit through your head on any given day is impressive, chaos."

"I'm just impressed you've caught on so quick to the fact that it is fictional-boyfriend material. And while I may enjoy a sprint through a dark and dangerous fictional world, I'm not sure what I think of it actually becoming a reality."

He places a warm, steady hand on my thigh and offers a light squeeze. "I promise I am not kidnapping you or leading you to any dark and dangerous areas. No crazed murder fantasies here."

I do laugh at that—at some of my words to him from that first time we met again in Havenwood. He'd been so concerned about me walking back to Reece's alone. If I'd had any idea of the trauma that triggered his reaction, would I have let him go with me?

"I can't believe you remember that."

"I remember everything about you."

As the truck rolls to a stop, I hear him shift it into park. "Can I take off these blinders now?"

"Give me two seconds to get everything set, and then I'll help you get out. Okay?"

"Okay, but if it takes more than three, I may have to assume that you are a serialist and that I need to take my chances and run."

"Smartass."

I stick my tongue out in response. As Noah's door clicks open then closed, I start to fidget.

Yes, I agreed to this date.

Yes, I want this thing—this relationship—to thrive.

But what if whatever he has planned proves we aren't as compatible as I think?

As my mind drifts to all the ways this could go horribly wrong, Noah startles me by opening the passenger door.

"Okay, miss. Let's get you situated a few feet over here and I'll remove the blindfold."

As he guides me along, I note the crunch of grass and leaves under my shoes. The air is fresh, and it's cool for a summer afternoon. I almost question him again but stop just as Noah brings my body into his, halting us. He slips the blindfold off and hugs my back to his front.

Staring in awe at the sight in front of me, I let myself lean into Noah's hold, unsure how to convey my thoughts to him.

It's perfect. Simple as that.

Noah's old truck is parked on a hill in one of the ranch's fields, a handful of horses grazing nearby. We're far enough away from town that it's quiet out, the noise pollution not reaching us. "What do you think, gorgeous? Worthy of a book boyfriend's first date?"

All I can manage is an enthusiastic nod as I step closer to the tailgate, taking in the dozen blankets and pillows that create a comfortable snuggle spot in the bed of his truck. A speaker is situated on the tire well, the low hum of some old-town country floating through.

"You did all this for me?"

I squeal as he lifts me up into the bed, not expecting the sudden move but loving it all the same. He slides in next to me and slips his arm around me.

"I wanted to run through the town square screaming 'Jett Taylor is my girl' at the top of my lungs, but I figured that'd have you fleeing Havenwood and the town questioning what little sanity I possess."

"Fair enough," I say, unable to sort through my thoughts. This is the most thought-out, put-together date I've ever been on.

"We have subs from Jace's place, dessert from the future home of The Write Brew, and Dr. Pepper. Also, plenty of blankets to snuggle in even if I'm partial to being snuggled instead," says Noah.

"You are very snuggable," I say, leaning into his side.

His arm wraps around me, tucking in at my waist and gently running a finger over the skin at the hem of my shirt. My head rests in the space between his neck and shoulder so naturally that I wonder how I ever thought Joey and I were right for each other.

Loving Noah is like breathing in fresh air for the first time.

Being loved by Noah? That shit is insane.

I never expected to find a man who trusts me implicitly, who understands and caters to my needs, or who wants me to succeed more than I do. Three-in-one package deal.

Tilting my chin until I can see his profile, I can't help but grin. "I love you, Noah."

He glances down and reaches his free hand to cup my cheek. His thumb glides along my lip before he leans in and gently teases my lips with his. As he sits back, the full grin on his face lights his eyes.

"I'll never tire of hearing you say that. I love you, too. More than I ever thought I could."

And while his lips tip into a gorgeous smile, there is still a shadow that flits across his expression. He doesn't try to hide it from me, and that willingness to be vulnerable grounds me. The fact that I recognize it, but also the realization that no man has ever allowed me to witness his emotions from me.

"What do you need, Noah?"

"I'm good. I swear."

"No. You're always making sure I have what I need, whether I see it or not. You tend to do it for everyone without even noticing that you're doing it. Drew, Kelsey, Declan. You're our caretaker. Well, you and Jace. We all see it. Maybe I have missed some of the cues up until recently, but even I can see how much you've been struggling. You're great at hiding it, but there's this shadow in your eyes. There has been since February." My hands cradle his cheeks, forcing him to look me in the eye as I say, "You're the one who is always saying this town is all about helping others. Let them help. Let me help."

"I'm fine, chaos." His eyes flit away from mine before closing.

"Don't lie to me, elevator man."

This man is everything to me, and he's clearly still trying to be the caretaker. But sooner or later, he'll realize that I've made my decision. I'm done running, and I know what I want. Or rather, *who* I want.

Leaning his head back against the rear window of the truck, he blindly reaches for my hand and squeezes it. I squeeze back, hopefully lending him the confidence to say whatever he's thinking.

"I made an appointment with Kristen. I want to be able to give you the freedom you deserve. Logically, I know you should be able to walk around town without me needing to bubble wrap you or place myself between you and the road. I want to make sure my grief doesn't suffocate you or hold you back. I don't want to ever be a controlling asshat who loses sight of how lucky he is, so I'm going to work on me."

"You'd never hold me back, Noah. All you've done since we met is push me to strive for things I never thought I'd accomplish."

He cuts me off from saying more. "Yeah, but what if I do? What if, at some point down the road, I let my constant worry for your safety keep you from opening a second location, or traveling, or something else you set your heart on?"

"Honey, I think the fact that you worry about the what-ifs is a pretty strong indicator that you won't do any of that. You love fiercely. You worry because you care." I snuggle deeper into his chest while pulling a blanket up to my chin. "I'm proud of you for talking to someone, but I've never once felt like you were overstepping."

He kisses the top of my head, a deep sigh releasing some of the tension in his posture. We sit in silence, taking comfort in the closeness while soaking in the view. As the sun starts to set, pink and orange dance across the sky, bathing the horses and the field in a soft glow. It's peaceful out here, as if none of life's problems can reach us.

I nuzzle back into that perfect divot at Noah's shoulder and breathe in his teakwood scent. This is perfect. He's perfect. Havenwood, too.

There's just one thing missing from this crazy new life of mine. And if Noah can be brave enough to tackle his demons, then so can I. It's time to repair the last broken piece.

CHAPTER TWENTY-EIGHT

Jett

Oakley: Noah says you're the reason he's talking to someone.

Jett: It was all him.

Oakley: Doubtful…Thank you.

Oakley: Do you love him?

Jett: I do. Never imagined finding my own book boyfriend after reading so many.

> Jett: Sweet little small town romance.

> Oakley: Knight in shining armor = elevator mechanic covered in carbon dust.

> Jett: …or a guy in pads and skates?

> Oakley: That ship has sailed.

> Jett: Mhmm. Whatever you say, friend.

The drive into the city limits seems to take twice as long as it used to. It must be because of the black, anxiety-ridden hole growing in the pit of my stomach. This is probably the most impulsive thing I've done in at least a month. Now that I think about it, I haven't had nearly the hair-trigger on my impulses since moving to Havenwood.

Parking in front of a large ranch home complete with a white picket fence, I take a breath and force the anxiety to settle. I need to do this.

You are worthy of love.

You deserve love.

You deserve happiness.

Embrace the chaos.

The last of those repeats in my head, Noah's voice a soothing reminder that I am strong and capable as I knock on the front door and wait for it to open.

As the rustic door creaks, an older version of me peers around the frame. Same bright-green eyes, same fine, brown hair but with some gray mixed in.

"Jett?" my mother asks, pure confusion lining her face.

"Hey, Mama." Shifting my weight back and forth, I bite my lip. "Any chance we can talk for a few minutes?"

She shakes off the shock of seeing me on her doorstep for the first time in who knows how long and opens the door wider. "Of course. Sorry, I was expecting it to be the twins and their friend coming home from rehearsals. They left their keys on the counter this morning. Come in. We can chat in the family room."

As I follow her into the airy room and take a seat on the couch, pictures snag my attention. I never lived here, but the photographic evidence would suggest otherwise. Ones of me and Reece. Family shots of us and both parents. Even more of Anna and Calla, understandably. This house is a place of love. A home.

Just not my home.

My home is an hour away with a man who loves me, lifts me up every day, and pushes me to chase my dreams. Being able to finally recognize that sends a wave of emotion straight to my heart.

Havenwood is my home.

"Jett? Are you alright, sweetie?" Mom's concerned voice draws my focus back to why I hopped in my car and drove two towns over without much—if any—of a plan.

"Yeah. Sorry, I just got lost in the thought of how good this season of life is turning out to be." I wait for the usual annoyance of my wandering mind to settle on her face, but it never comes. Instead, a small smile lifts one side of her lips.

"You always did do that. I'm surprised you never wrote your own books. Your imagination certainly was expansive enough."

My body suddenly feels unbalanced, similar to an anxiety attack. And yet, I know that isn't what this is. Did I let my emotions and personal struggles color how I viewed my mother's reactions? That small piece of me that is so used to running at the smallest sign of confrontation itches to book it from this house. Four months ago, I would have. Hell, I wouldn't have made the drive to see her at all.

Suddenly bashful, I peek through my lashes at my mother. "You would have supported me in something like that? Something that has no guarantee of success?" Worrying at the hem of my shirt, I hold my breath while waiting for her answer.

Whatever she sees in my expression has her moving to the cushion next to me, the leather dipping as she settles in. Mama takes my hands and places them in her lap, covering them with her own. "Jennette Marie, we may have a more...strained...relationship than your brother and I do, but I have and will *always* support your endeavors. Whatever they may be. Even if they may not pan out how you expect."

Wringing my hands together as her words hit home, I decide to go for it. It's now or never, and having both parents on board would make The Write Brew all the more special.

"Here's the thing, Mama."

As I fill her in on what Noah, Kelsey, and I have been working toward, the excitement that comes from talking about my passion bubbles to the surface. The ability to talk freely as my mother's own excitement shines in her eyes erases the last bit of anxiety about sharing this with her.

Maybe I've gone years without seeing eye to eye with her. Maybe it was misplaced confusion or just plain old poor communication, but the idea that my mom is proud of what I am accomplishing is the icing on the cake. And I want her to experience the finished project.

"Our ribbon cutting ceremony is two weeks from Saturday. I know the twins may already have plans but—"

Her hand lands on my thigh and squeezes. "I wouldn't miss it for the world, Jett. I'll be there."

Tears prick the backs of my eyes, and for once, I let them fall. The relief and pure joy at her response sends my emotions into overdrive. As her arms wrap snuggly around me, the quiet sniffles turn to sobs.

"It's all right, precious. Let it out. Mama's here," she murmurs over and over, her fingers expertly running through my hair that she somehow managed to slip from its tie.

I finally run out of tears by the time the door opens and Anna and Calla slip inside with another lithe preteen by their sides. I quickly wipe the remaining tears from my face, but I'm sure the red and swollen look gives it away. To their credit, neither girl mentions it.

"Jett! What are you doing here? Are you staying for dinner?" Calla, the oldest of the two, asks as she slams her body into mine seconds before Anna does the same on my other side. Neither of them can be more than one hundred pounds soaking wet, but their strength is impressive.

"Hey, girls. Wasn't planning on it, but..." I glance at Mama for guidance.

When she smiles and nods with moisture in her own eyes, I relent.

"I guess driving on a full stomach *would* be better than eating the crackers in my car."

The girls squeal as our mom directs them and their friend upstairs to freshen up.

"You just made their day, Jett."

Shrugging off the thanks, I stuff my hands in my pockets. "I'll try to do better about coming around. For them, I mean. I know they see Reece pretty regularly."

"They'd love that, but do what you need to do for you, okay?"

As the three girls run back down the stairs and into the kitchen, we follow the sounds of laughter and prepare a meal...as a family. And when my step-father comes in, we sit and eat the first non-awkward family dinner I've had since before my parents' divorce.

Is it too much to hope that this can become my new normal?

CHAPTER TWENTY-NINE

Noah

Today is the day.

Our entire friend group is here to help Jett make sure everything is in place. Kelsey's color selection was spot on with Jett's dream layout. The dark-stained wood bookshelves are lined with a small selection of romance novels by some of the authors Jett has worked with.

Everyone she reached out to was thrilled to be a part of this. And almost all of them have asked to work with Jett in an editorial capacity again now that whatever projects they'd been working on previously are complete. She broke down in tears when she realized she'd have to put people on a waitlist.

Even now, as I step into her back and wrap my arms around her, she seems at a loss for words. Like she can't believe this is really happening.

"You did it, chaos. In less than thirty minutes, you get to cut the ribbon and open the doors to this amazing creation of yours."

Her head swishes back and forth. "Not mine. We did this. You. Kelsey. Our friends."

"Our family did this," I say as she leans up to kiss along my jaw.

"Our family. Still gives me chills, but it's true. Isn't it?"

It is. Our little band of misfit siblings would do anything for one another, much like this town. We take care of our own, and a product of that philosophy is about to open its doors to the community.

As we bask in each other and the reality that Jett is finally doing what she's always wanted, Kelsey walks up and joins our embrace. I think she's more excited than Jett at this point.

"Jett? It's time," she squeals.

Jett smiles, but I can see the edge of worry. Squeezing her one more time, I try to sooth some of those fears. "You've got this, gorgeous. This town is one hundred percent behind you. They are just as excited for this rebranding as we are."

Glancing out the front window, she winces. "Don't think I expected literally everyone to show up for this, though."

Kelsey hears her and hollers across the room. "We got this, babe!"

Tilting her chin up with my thumb, I wait until she makes eye contact. "She's right, you know? We are all here, ready to celebrate. And I'm pretty sure I saw some important individuals out in the crowd earlier."

Her eyes widen at that. She knew her mom was coming, but we also managed to get her dad down from Kentucky without her knowing. He's supported her in this since she was a kid. It's only right that he can be here for the grand opening.

After a few more deep breaths, Jett finally walks to the door and steps outside with our entire crew following her. She glances around, taking in the crowded sidewalk and street, and I can see the moment she almost bolts. Her entire body tenses, and she takes a step backward.

Instead, she looks to me. And man, if that isn't the biggest boost to my ego. I silence this girl's chaos for her when she needs it. Doing my best to exude confidence, I guess it works, because Jett takes a steadying breath before smiling and looking back at our community.

"This is so beyond my comfort zone, so just bear with me for a minute." The crowd quiets as Jett settles into the role of business owner. "I know most people in this town have figured out that I'm Reece's little sister. You've probably realized that I'm a little odd, talk to myself, shy away from the crowds and conversation. And yet, none of you have shied away from me. No one has called me out or picked at me for being myself. This town truly lives up to its name of being a haven to anyone looking for a fresh start, and I couldn't be prouder to call this place home."

She motions behind her at the new logo on the window. "This dream of mine became a reality thanks to the relationships I've built since January. From a grumpy mechanic who refused to give up on me, to a friendship with the town baker that turned into an unexpected business relationship. I couldn't be more excited to introduce you guys to The Write Brew, co-owned by Kelsey Riley."

Cheers erupt from the crowd, and the energy is infectious. Jett and Kelsey are both nearly bouncing in their shoes.

Kelsey addresses the crowd one more time. "We are so excited you're here! Now, please. Come inside, browse, and enjoy some of the delicious pastries that we concocted specifically for today."

As everyone begins to make their way inside, I catch Reece's eye from the other side of the crowd. A man who I know from pictures is their dad is with him. Reece nods in acknowledgment and steers them—and their mom, I realize—toward the entrance where Jett and Kelsey are greeting everyone.

Quickly slipping inside, I wrap my arms around Jett and lean down to her ear.

"There are a few special guests here to see you."

She looks up at me in confusion, but I let my eyes wander to where her family is walking through the door. I keep my hands on her hips as she follows my line of sight. When she realizes who it is, she looks back and forth between them and me in disbelief. Gently kissing her forehead, I nudge her in their direction.

"Go see your dad, chaos. He may be more excited than the rest of us."

Tears begin to gather in her eyes as her emotions war within. "How?" she asks, stepping back into me. "I talked to him last week, and he didn't think he'd be able to get away."

I swipe the pad of my thumb across her cheekbone, gathering the lone tear that escapes.

"Your brother made some calls when I told him."

"You and Reece working together?"

"Anything for you."

Her kiss is quick and sweet before she's rushing toward her family.

"Daddy!" As she slings herself into her arms, I make the rounds, ensuring everything is still running smoothly.

As I'm replenishing the first of many empty cookie plates, Kristen walks over.

"You guys finally did it, yeah?" She smiles. While she is the town therapist, she's also a really good friend. Talking to her has helped both me and Jett work through some of our past struggles.

"She's worked her butt off for this, Kris. It's thanks to you, you know."

Kristen shakes her head in denial, but we all know it's true. If she hadn't had an opening that first day that Jett called, she'd have never moved down here.

"Well, I'm not here on official business. I'm here strictly as a friend. I feel like I don't ever get to chat with the outside world anymore, and Jett only comes in once a month."

"We're both glad you could be here. Seriously, Kristen. Maybe you and Declan should join us some when we all get together at Riley's. Like old times."

"I'd like that. Not sure I can get the two stubborn Flynn boys to agree, but I'll do my best."

"All I can ask," I say before she walks off. As I turn to grab another empty tray, I nearly bump into Jett. She grabs my hand and pulls me behind her, walking toward the back office. When I open my mouth to ask what is going on, she shushes me. As she closes the door behind us, I expect her to talk.

Instead, she pushes my back into the door, jumps, and wraps her legs around my waist. My hands settle under her thighs as her lips find mine easily, and I let her control the kiss. It's her usual close-mouthed sweet kiss but with so much passion, I'm worried she may light us on fire.

As she backs off and rests her forehead against mine, I watch as a jumble of emotions rush across her face before settling on one: pure joy.

"Not that I'm complaining. Far from it. But what was that for?" I ask against her lips. I swear then and there that I'll do anything to keep this happiness alive.

She shakes her head but smiles, that lip of hers nipped between her teeth. "Elevator mechanic. Caretaker extraordinaire. Chaos coordinator in every sense of the word. I'm never giving you up, Noah Slater." She kisses me again before dropping to her feet.

"Mmm. Never get tired of kissing you, chaos." I find her lips once more before moving away from the door and opening it. "But we should probably get back out to your grand opening, yeah?"

She nods, the grin still plastered to her face as she slips her fingers back into mine.

I don't think life can get any better than this.

CHAPTER THIRTY

Jett

As my brain comes into consciousness, I silently groan.

Today is not the day. Another cramp rolls through. The misery of day one menstrual cramps is excessively painful. It must be a design flaw. Because why on God's green Earth would he have purposely designed a body that *sheds its uterine lining*. Painfully. Once. A. Month. Like, no thank you. Please return it and provide me with a new, better-functioning organ, please.

I pull my phone from under my pillow, having forgotten to charge it again, before curling into a tight ball and completely disappearing under the comforter on Noah's bed. Sadie shifts against my feet. Since our truck bed date, it seems like we've unofficially moved in together. It's both parts terrifying and exhilarating. It feels like we've moved so fast, but at the same time, we've been on this path for roughly five months now. Everything with Noah is just so seamless.

Once I tuck my knees all the way to my chest and wait for Sadie to settle in at my back, I check my phone. There is another text from my mom and a "good morning beautiful" text from Noah, complete with a sunrise picture from the roof of whatever building he is working at today.

I start to send a response when my phone rings, my mom's photo popping up on the screen. Sighing and hoping I don't live to regret it, I tap the green answer button.

"Hello?" My voice is twinged with discomfort, and I bite my lip and pray that she doesn't notice.

"Jett," my mom starts, clearly surprised that I answered. Can't blame her. While things aren't as rocky as they were, I'm still not joining Reece for his weekly calls with her. I also may or may not have been communicating through text only.

"Honey, I didn't expect you to answer."

"I know," I say shortly, a cramp ripping through my defenses.

"What's wrong, honey? You sound pained."

My filter is officially gone because I mutter "monthly stuff" without hesitation before facepalming myself for blabbing.

"Do you have someone around to help you out?"

"Mom, no. I'm fine." I try to placate her, but her mom senses must be more powerful, because she reads right through it.

"Certainly not. You sound miserable, honey. I'll be there in an hour." With that, she ends the call, and I'm stuck wondering what the hell just happened.

> Jett: Mom's on her way to Havenwood.

> Reece: What? Why?

> Jett: Answered the phone without thinking.

> Slipped that it's Cramp Camp over here.

> Reece: Shit. You ok? About both aspects.

> Jett: Intervention would be cool. Not sure how long I'll last.

***

Before I can get comfortable on the couch, my phone goes off again, Noah's name lighting up the screen.

"Hey."

"You okay, chaos?" His concern has butterflies filling my stomach for a moment.

"What do you mean?"

"Your brother just texted me telling me I needed to cause a distraction for you later if you still have company."

I roll my eyes. Of course, Reese pulled it onto Noah.

"My mom's coming down. I asked for help to get her gone later if it turns out to be too much to handle. Not sure of my mental capacity today."

"Need me to come home?" he asks. Not me silently loving how we've taken to referring to our two lofts as "home."

My eyes pinch closed as another bout of pain overtakes my middle, the smallest whimper slipping through my lips. Too late, I realize Noah hears it.

"Jett? I can be home in forty-five minutes. Just say the word."

"No, um. Just girl stuff." My cheeks heat with embarrassment, even though he's proven not to be affected by talk of cycles.

I hear him sigh in relief that it is nothing more than that.

"I'm sorry, gorgeous. Today is your day off, right? Get some rest, and I'll pick up anything you need on my way home. Just text me a list of what you want."

"You don't need to, Noah."

"Didn't say anything about me, now did I? If you don't send me a list, I'll just go get random things that sound good, and you can't hold me accountable for any of the random shit I bring you."

"Okay, okay," I say softly. "Same things as last month please."

"Animal crackers, peanut butter cups, and Twizzlers. Got it. Try to get some rest, sweet girl. I love you."

"Love you, too, Noah."

The feel of the words is still so new and makes me feel all the feels. Though that could also be due to the crazy influx of hormones.

"If you think of anything you need, just text me."

"Okay, dear."

I can hear the smile in his voice as he parts ways.

"See you later, chaos. Give Sadie ear scratches for me."

With a bit of luck, I manage to doze back off. When I wake again, it is to incessant pounding on the front door and Sadie barking. Except the knocking is not on Noah's door. It's on mine, next door.

"Shit," I mumble as I stumble out of the covers.

Sadie is already at the door, complaining loudly in her own way and stomping her nails against the hardwoods.

"Quiet, girl. Sit."

She sits, but the wiggle butt ensues, whines and whimpers filling the air in her excitement for me to open the door. Curled in on myself as I try to keep the pain to a minimum, I unlock and open the door, peaking out. Sure enough, my mother is pounding on the door to my loft. Reece must have given her the address.

"Mom, you're banging on the wrong door," I whisper-yell.

She turns abruptly, startled by my voice. "Oh, Jett," she says as she quickly closes the short distance between us and wraps me into a hug. "Sorry, I thought that was your place."

"Technically." I blush. "I'm staying at Noah's."

Mom's eyes light up, and I can see two thousand questions brewing, but she keeps them to herself and ushers me back through the door.

"Come on, get back inside and I'll fix you up," she says as she nearly pushes me back through the door and closes it behind us. It's then that I notice the bags with her.

"You didn't need to drive down here, Mom. It's like a half-hour drive one way. I'm fine," I lie, wishing desperately that I was curled back up under the fluffy comforter in Noah's room.

"Hush, you. Go put on one of your shows and curl up." She waves me off with her hands, guiding me toward the couch. "I'll get you some ginger ale and animal crackers before I start getting the hot water bottle prepared."

Mom takes care of what she says, and I return to bed, not interested in turning on the television. When my mother waltzes in with my water jug filled to the brim with ice and ginger ale, a bowl of animal crackers, and both ibuprofen and acetaminophen options, I can't take the questions swirling around in my head anymore.

"What made you come, Mom?"

"I know things are a little strained between us, but you're still my baby." She leans forward and rests her hand on my multi-blanket covered knee. "Reece also filled me in on your romance. He must not have realized that you wouldn't be at your own home when he sent me the address earlier."

"Yeah, that part is really new." I feel myself wanting to shy away at the admission but force myself to own it. There is nothing wrong with doing what makes me happy. "Reece doesn't know about the sharing of lofts yet."

"I brought lavender candles and bubble bath. Can I interest you in that?"

"Probably after I pop something for the pain." The level of exhaustion that I feel is top notch. No way this is just from my period. As I try to think on what could have me this exhausted, I realize that it's most likely a combination of the crazy changes over the last few months as well as the fact that we stayed up until almost one in the morning watching a west coast hockey game.

Mom slips down the hall to the bathroom and starts running bath water.

"You don't need to pamper me, Mom. I can do this part myself," I holler after her, but she keeps at it.

"Let your mama take care of her baby, why don't you?"

Instead of arguing as she slips back into the bedroom, I ask shyly, "Did you make a way for me to fall asleep without slipping down?"

"I sure did. Go enjoy it. We can talk about your boyfriend and the address change after you get a nap in."

As I sink into the bubble bath, the lavender candle's aroma surrounding me in the small bathroom, I silently thank my mother for her nosy, excessive need to take care of me even when I make it absolutely impossible for her to do so. Sadie settles on the rug beside the bath, and I rest my head on the headrest of towels that Mom folded for me.

I don't know how much I doze, but the water has cooled when I come to. There are clean clothes and one of Noah's sweatshirts resting on the counter with a pair of purple fuzzy socks on top. As I move through the motions of drying off and redressing, a small part of me dreads the thought of drying my hair. Instead of dealing with it, I towel dry and pull it into a knot on top of my head.

About the time that I realize Sadie isn't with me, I notice two voices talking down the hall. Picking up my pace, I nearly run to the kitchen and sling myself into Noah's already open arms.

"Hey, gorgeous. How ya' feelin'?" he asks. His hand immediately starts its trek up and down my spine in a soothing motion as he drops a kiss on my forehead.

"Better thanks to Mama's intervention. What are you doing home?" When I look up, he smirks at me before looking at my mom. Her gentle smile has me looking back and forth between mother and boyfriend. "What's going on with you two? This is kind of creepy, to be honest."

Noah chuckles before pulling an envelope from his back pocket. "I left work early so I could pick up this," he says while placing the envelope into my hand.

Glancing up at him through my lashes, I suddenly feel bashful. "What is it?"

"Open it and find out," he says.

"You'll love it," my mom adds, stepping close and squeezing my shoulder. "I'm going to slip out since you are no longer alone."

Reaching out to grab her hand, I hold tight, unable to voice my appreciation.

"Love you, sweetheart. Call or text me, okay?"

I mumble an "I love you" and stare after her as she leaves. Once the door latches, my attention flips back to Noah and what is in my hand.

Feeling even more unsure, I slowly peel into the envelope and slide its contents onto the counter. Leaning my hip into the bar stool, I stare down at two season passes for the Steele Valley Voltage's upcoming season.

"Is this for real? How did you even manage this?" My fingers ghost over the items in front of me. These haven't gone on sale yet. When I say as much, Noah reaches up to smooth my lip from between my teeth.

"I had Silas pull some strings for me. He was more than willing when I told him they were for the woman of my dreams."

"Stop."

"Seriously. That's all it took."

"This is too much, Noah. I know what those tickets run. I've looked at them every year but never had anyone to go with." Unable to keep my fidgeting under wraps, I pick at my sleeve. Noah quickly traps my hands in his and places them on his chest.

"I called in favors, so I didn't pay full price. But I would have if I hadn't been able to secure these."

"You're insane."

"For you? Always."

Fisting his shirt and pulling him closer, I press my lips to Noah's. He understands my method of appreciation and kisses me back, one hand sliding to cradle my head while the other settles on my waist.

My mind drifts, wondering how any of this is real.

This chapter of life since moving to Havenwood was a much-needed reset. I never expected to find love, friendships, or business success when I came down here on a whim after being stuck in an elevator during a thunder storm. I never expected Noah Slater and this town to piece me back together the way they did. For the first time in my adult life, I feel whole.

Fighting the sudden emotions that these thoughts bring, I pull back just enough to ask, "How did you do it?"

"Do what?"

"Turn my life around. Quiet my mind. Make me a better, stronger version of myself."

"That was all you, chaos. You learned how to chase your dreams. I just cheered you on." He squeezes me to his chest, his chin resting on my head. "And I'll continue being here for you for as long as you'll let me."

Lucky for me, I plan on letting him be my biggest fan indefinitely.

Epilogue

NOAH

"**B**ut like, are you *sure* you want to deal with this long-term? I mean, I know it's been almost ten months—not that I'm counting or anything—and you've learned the doom pile system, but at some point, you're going to get sick of me. You have to."

I swear I could strangle this girl if I didn't love her so much. The way her brain works is anyone's guess, and I am at a loss as to how to get it through to her that she is my end game.

"Chaos, you are shit out of luck. I'm not going anywhere."

"But you might. I put peanut butter crackers in the freezer and a container of gelato in the refrigerator, for cryin' out loud."

As she tosses the ruined dessert into the trash can, I refrain from telling her that it should be fine to put it in the freezer now. She'd argue that the texture is ruined. It's alright. I have my own stash next door specifically for her.

"I want it all with you, Jett. Don't you get that?" I ask as I try to take her hand into mine, but she pulls away.

"No! I don't get it, Noah. I am a disaster in every sense of the word. What could you possibly—"

I cut her off. "Precisely. You, Jennette Marie Taylor, are walking, talking, beautiful chaos, and I want nothing more than to call you mine."

God, why can this girl not grasp how absolutely perfect she is?

Jett's eyes widen as I reach into the pocket of my jeans and pull out a small box before extending my closed fist to her. She hesitantly reaches out to grasp her surprise.

"You are not proposing, are you? Please say no. I mean, you would make for a great husband and I love you and want that at some point, but I doubt either of us are ready for that level of commitment and—"

Her words end as abruptly as they began as she takes in what is resting in my open palm. Because there, in the center of my oil-stained, calloused hand, is a tiny decorative storage box painted to look like the special edition cover of her all-time favorite romance novel.

"It is absolutely beautiful," she whispers as she gingerly lifts it from my palm as if it'll fall apart if she touches it wrong.

"It won't break, chaos. It's made of cedar. Hand crafted and hand painted for your bookshelf. Or wherever else you might want to put it."

Her lower lip trembles, and I start to panic. "Please don't cry—this is supposed to make you happy. Not tearful."

She lets loose a wet laugh. "I can be both, damn it."

"Open it."

"It opens?" she squeaks, but she is already lifting the cover to reveal the small storage space that I had created within it. Resting in the center of it is a key to my loft.

Her moist eyes meet mine, the traces of a grin tugging at the corner of her mouth. "Is this what I think it is?"

"Nothing needs to be rushed. If you only want to move one shirt a week until every item of yours has moved in, then that is fine with me. I just want you in my bed every night. What do you say?"

Her lip trembles before she grasps it between her teeth and nods excitedly. "Hell yes, Noah."

Acknowledgements

If you've made it this far, then thank you from the bottom of my heart for giving Jett and Noah a chance.

I started this journey in November 2023 with zero expectations for anyone to read it but me. Jett and Noah were supposed to be a standalone book with no chance of continuing as a series. Instead, they inserted themselves into the fictional world I've been building since I was fifteen.

One of the most deserving of a thank you is my editor, Andrea. I could not have done this without you. Your suggestions dating all the way back to the beta read helped make this book possible.

My cover would not have been possible without the fabulous talent of Acacia at Ever After Cover Design. I couldn't have given any less detail or direction, and she still managed to create this beauty on the first try.

To anyone who viewed the earliest versions of this story and became a cheerleader, thank you.

Lastly, a big thank you to my husband for putting up with all the late-night writing sessions and for answering any elevator questions I had.

Thank you for reading!

Want more of Jett and Noah? Join my newsletter for sneak peeks and updates on the next installment of the Havenwood crew.

Or follow me on social media:

Instagram: @emchandler.books

TikTok: @emchandler.author

YouTube and Pinterest: @emchandlerbooks

Website: www.emchandlerbooks.com

www.ingramcontent.com/pod-product-compliance
Lightning Source LLC
Chambersburg PA
CBHW050022120726
47903CB00006B/1874